The Duty and the Dream

....

Abigale Schmidt

Copyright © 2025 by Abigale Schmidt

All rights reserved.

No portion of this book may be reproduced in any form without written permission from the publisher or author, except as permitted by U.S. copyright law.

Contents

1. Chapter 1 — 1
2. Chapter 2 — 9
3. Chapter 3 — 19
4. Chapter 4 — 25
5. Chapter 5 — 32
6. Chapter 6 — 38
7. Chapter 7 — 50
8. Chapter 8 — 59
9. Chapter 9 — 70
10. Chapter 10 — 76
11. Chapter 11 — 83
12. Chapter 12 — 92
13. Chapter 13 — 99
14. Chapter 14 — 104
15. Chapter 15 — 109

16.	Chapter 16	114
17.	Chapter 17	129
18.	Chapter 18	138
19.	Chapter 19	150
20.	Epilogue	154

Chapter 1

He was once again walking in the coldest parts of the world. Not only did he want to avoid the sun but he wanted to feel the cold harshness bite into his skin. He wanted the cold to gnaw at his bones and he wanted more than anything to be brought by down the ice in the air. He wanted to be overcome by weakness, to be dragged down to the floor like a mortal and to be forced to struggle for life.

But Joseph wasn't weak. He wasn't born to be weak and he had not been raised to be weak. He had been trained, he had seen things, he had done things that meant he wasn't weak no matter how he begged the world around him for such a luxury. Weakness meant he could get away from who he was, that someone would save him instead of him having to save everyone else. He wanted to scream at the world for the horror he saw and the horror he was.

Two weeks ago Lily had given birth to her fourth child, a little boy and the babe's blue eyes were so bright they had pierced Joseph. They had seemed to look into his very heart and like the other three had not managed to do, this fourth one had made him realise what a monster he was. And he didn't have to be. But it was now in his very blood.

It wasn't the cold that brought him to his knees, it was a weakness of some kind, but his training made it so that even as he fell to his knees his back remained ram rod straight. His head was raised and his eyes stared forward. He bowed to no one. He bent his back for no one and as his knees touched the frosted ground he did not shiver. He showed no one the things that got to him. He screamed out, a terrible rumbling sound of anger. He let rip the emotions building and boiling inside of himself. He was a lonely vampire, he had fought in so many wars and he was a leader of so many regiments they literally called him now only when they went into battle. His tactics, his undeniable skill made it so they all called to him. He told them where to go, how to fight and left them with his instructions while he won the battles for him.

He simply was good at what he was taught. An orphan himself, the lack of parental guidance had forced him into the world alone and despite his cousin's influence and parents he had walked away from them; they were the family he wanted but could not have. He isolated himself from them and Perttu never gave up on him. But Joseph gave up on himself when he understood what he was becoming.

Houses infront of him with their lights shining were like a beacon. Like fire in the pitch black of a forest they drew him in so his knees left the floor and his powerful figure was walking towards the life and warmth. He couldn't stop himself from walking on; he didn't really understand why he was entertaining this whim of his. He usually ignored what he wanted and went about in a cold and heartless manner to his destination. His life was one of battle, he travelled to get to battle and once won he travelled to the next. Never before had the light shining from a bedroom peaked his attention.

His wandering feet led him to a village, a well off and yet not upper class sort of village. He turned his head abruptly at the sound of laughter coming from the town hall. There must be a gathering of some sort, the mortals did love to have organised dances together where they showed off their status. He shook his head, the skirts those women wore were cumbersome and annoying to him, he hated being around mortal women in such skirts, the vampire women managed both modesty and advantage very well.

He shook his head wandering forward to the town hall and heard the violins playing there. They were high pitched, fast played; a waltz if he wasn't mistaken. He shook his head again, he had never mastered the art of dance, he had had no father to teach him when the time had been appropriate and had ran away from Perttu and his father when they tried to teach him. The privilege had been his fathers, no one else's in order to teach him and with no father he had dropped the idea of ever dancing.

Sweet giggling over took his thoughts and he eyed the door as a woman was stood outside leaning against the doorway accompanied with another man. He felt his rage blossoming in his chest. His teeth grew. Why was he so angry?

"Mark, I like dancing with you, I really do but what would Camilla say?"

"I don't care for Camilla."

"Sure you do, you look at her every five minutes."

"Elsa, please."

"Am I making you blush with my acute sense of observation?" She taunted and Joseph felt himself calming under the tone of her voice. It was playful and light. His teeth shrank back down to a human length and the hair standing to attention on his arm slowly began to flatten back out.

"I will never get Camilla. She had many suitors."

"Of course she does, but she has yet to accept one of them. If you never try you will never know Mark and time is running out. She is eighteen already and to be married by the summer. Her father wants her a wife before he passes away and he is getting more ill by the day."

"She will reject me."

"She may not."

"What do I do if she does?"

"What will you do if she does not?"

The blonde haired beauty standing in the doorway had her curled hair pinned back and wore no make up on face that would have otherwise have taken away her natural beauty. It was that very beauty that caused Joseph to hide in the shadows. He was a man hardened by his years in battle and he had no smooth lines, his skin was not soft and the lines that etched into his face told of years of struggle. This beautiful girl infront of him was flawless. He was both drawn to her and desperate to stay away from her so that even in his human form - the subtler image of him - he still was not able to be a man suitable for her. Imagine him in his beast form. As a true vampire.

Her head snapped up, he cursed himself, he hadn't been careful to move slower. She had caught his movement and he closed his eyes. Women; not only where their dresses annoying but one was now distracting him to the point of being seen when he had the skill to avoid such a thing.

"Go on Mark, go on in and try your luck with her. If you're to be married for the rest of your life why not have it be with the girl of your dreams."

"I shouldn't leave you out here alone."

"I am fine. Go, stop putting it off any longer."

Joseph bore witness to her putting a delicate gloved hand on the man's shoulder and encouraging him to go inside to the woman he wanted to be with. Just that little gesture awakened a yearning in him, deep inside, to have someone touch him. Touch him in a way of kindness, love even, as opposed to touching him to kill him or wound him. He had gotten that from Perttu on occasion when they embraced each other as men before battle but the last time was years ago. He had gotten cuddles from Perttu's children but he tried to avoid it. It hurt to see such carefree innocence. It made him long to hold them tighter, closer to him when they wrapped their arms around his legs or waist. He wanted to hold them like they were his own but they were too weak to hold tighter. They were only children and he was scared of squashing them so he stayed away from them for their safety.

But now; seeing that casual gesture, he longed for one similar. He longed for his woman and he wanted the blonde haired beauty to be that woman. So much so he edged out his foot from the side of the building he was currently hiding in. He could not have her though. For the first time in many, many hundreds of years Joseph bowed his head and looked to the floor as he walked away from her. The grass was already crunched under his feet from people walking all over it. It was dark out but to him he saw the advantage of night. It offered a surplus of opportunity to hide and seek prey. The moon looked down on him lighting up a path that he might follow. His only source of light was that pale, soft touch. He would leave the village he had stumbled upon, he needed to head back down south anyway to help in a war there.

Pulling his coat further around him he raised his head and stared in the direction he was aiming for. His destination. How he wished he had not carved out this life for himself. How he wished he was not a sought after warlord called upon to win the battles other vampires were in adept to do.

"Why are you not at the ball?"

He stopped dead in his tracks. That voice, it was hers.

"I am not from around here."

"Why are you here then?"

"Go back inside, it is dangerous to be outside at night unaccompanied."

"I am a grown women I can manage a little darkness. Will you not turn around and look at me?"

"I must be going."

"Why were you hiding?"

"I do not hide."

He heard another giggle, feminine, unrestrained and gentle.

"OK then, Sir, why then were you watching from the shadows?"

He turned then, when he knew the moon was shining just right to glance off him in a diagonal line; from left shoulder to right hip and avoiding his face like the plague. She would not see his features.

"You're a quiet one. I can't see your face but I can see your shoes. Why not come in and dance a song before you get on your way."

"I do not dance."

His voice was curt, abrupt and maybe a little harsh, it made the smile on this woman's face disappear and she looked at him properly.

"Well then good night Sir, it was a pleasure to speak to you. I must be getting back." He told himself it was what he wanted, what he needed to happen but he wasn't thinking straight. He wasn't in his right frame of mind, he especially knew he wasn't when the muslin of her gloves touched his palm and he felt the material.

What had he done? Her hand was in his and he had stopped her retreat. Her face gave neither displeasure nor anger, not even confusion away; it was simply patient, waiting for him to speak and explain why he stopped her. Now he loved the dress she wore. Now he thanked the heavens that she was wearing a skirt that flowed out and forced him to keep a little distance from her. If that dress had been in the style of the vampires he usually admired he would have gotten so close to her it would have ruined her reputation should someone come out from the town hall and see her in such proximity to him. She said nothing while she waiting for him only, her eyes they looked into his and pierced his soul. So alike to Perttu's fourth child. To Issai.

"What is your name?" He whispered.

"My name is Elsa, and yours?"

"Joseph."

"Are you sure Joseph, you will not join me for a dance. I assure I am good, I won't step on your toes."

"I did not lie when I said I did not dance. I am afraid I was never taught that. My apologies Miss, but I can not dance with you."

At his words she beamed at him, her white teeth on show and her ruby lips parted in such a manner as to render him stunned and fighting his urges.

"Then one day I should like to teach you. I have to be getting back now, they will notice my disappearance and I do not want to be caught outside..." She trailed off, looking a little embarrassed. He understood; to be seen with him would ruin her.

He nodded, "I will let you go Elsa, I will see you around. I will be in the village for the next week, I hope to see you in town on market day I usually get there when they are closing the stalls."

"See you on Tuesday then Joseph."

She went back inside and Joseph watched her go. Market day? Staying? What the hell had he just done? Why had he done it? He shook his head; great he would be braving the dusk light on Tuesday and he had would be in the company of mortal - all for one woman. One girl! He cursed whatever was going on in his messed up mind. He still watched as the last glimpse of golden blonde hair disappeared from the door frame and Elsa re-joined the party.

Chapter 2

He was furious, absolutely fuming at his stupidity. It wasn't dark yet and he was walking around on the streets. To make matters worse he had bought a suit! The night before he had decided that he wanted to look his best and now he was dressed in white and black – the colours of an elegant man of status – he walked with a cane down the streets. He looked pompous. A look he didn't care for and felt stupid to be seen as.

Growling in frustration he threw the cane to the side of the road where a beggar ran out and picked it up as if it were gold. Well the real silver top of it was worth quite a penny and the beggar was no doubt in for the treat of his life. He let the cane go, he hated holding it.

The collar of his shirt forced his head up and choked his throat. He felt constricted so he opened the first two buttons so the whole of his neck and maybe an inch further was on show. He had never been one to tuck his shirt in and he huffed as he untucked the white material from his black trousers. His tailored black coat still clung to his figure and the lapels of the jacket hid most of his untucked shirt so he suspected he wasn't too scruffy.

He had lacquered his hair back and he hated the look of it, so he walked over to the water fountain in the nearest park and stuck his head in it. He liked the coolness of the water on his overheated skin anyway. Hurriedly running his hands through his hair to rid himself of the sticky substance he stood up and let the water flick everywhere as he ran his fingers through the locks to mess them up; unintentionally gaining the attention of a group of upper class ladies. He ignored them.

All this worrying, all this expense on a suit and a silver topped cane for a lady he had decided he was not going to meet. He was due in the south and he wouldn't miss the battle. Animals like him were not meant for suits.

"My, what a show you just put on. Anyone would think you hated you new suit."

Whirling around he recognised that voice, thatm face. It was Elsa and she was staring at him with a smirk on her face.

"The suit isn't new."

The suit isn't new. If he was in a position to yell at himself for such a terrible opening sentence he would have. As it where the young woman in front of him was quietly laughing to herself and eyeing him up. He felt his cheeks heat up and he wondered what on earth had happened the war hardened soldier he once was. He felt like a hormonal teen boy at that moment.

"Well it looks very well kept." Was her reply. "I was wondering if you would still come today. I made an excuse especially to come to town. I insisted my papa buy me some hair ribbons, even though I have more than the shop itself."

"Well I am glad you came."

"Aren't you cold with your wet hair?"

"No."

Elsa was dying to laugh out loud. She had seen him walking on the streets with a face like he had just sucked on a lemon, lips pursed and cheeks hollow. He had looked incredibly stuck up until he threw aside his cane with a single swift move and it was sent flying across the very street. Taken aback by his abrupt bout of violence she had stared at him stunned, and then widened her eyes as he ripped open two buttons of his shirt and exposed his throat. To top it off he veered off from the road and proceeded to bend over a fountain and stick his very head in the water. So ungentlemanly like and yet it suited him.

She was hooked on his rough looking appearance and surprised that even though he didn't look like the gentlemen that she had been around he still had an air of elegance around him that told her she was speaking to an aristocrat.

"Well would you like to escort me to the ribbon shop?"

"Of course."

He offered his arm before he realised what it was he was doing. He was acting like a human. He should have turned around the minute he stepped on the street. He should have told her straight the other night that he wasn't staying and he should have proceeded to travel to the south. What he was doing now was wrong. He was purposely endangering this pretty and fragile human woman for a reason even he didn't know.

"It's a nice day today." She said trying desperately to start a conversation. He just looked at her, confused. It was cold for humans why would she say it was a nice day? What was this supposed to mean?

"It's cold."

"I'm making conversation."

"Oh."

Silence followed. He didn't understand how to make conversation. He had never really been in company where it was forced necessity to speak. He was used to the flow of conversation going on around him and pitching in only when it actually caught his attention or intrigued him. But he was in polite society and silences weren't favoured here. He took it as a sign that he was out of place and should leave. But he didn't.

"You're not very good on the conversation starting are you?"

"I have never had to be."

"Where are you from?"

"I was born two towns away from Hadrian's wall and since then have travelled all around the world."

"The world! That must be so exciting! Have you seen other cultures? And pretty ladies in their foreign dresses? Can you speak other languages?"

So that was how to start a conversation. "I've seen a fair bit but most of my time has been in war. I can speak a few languages."

"War? You are in the army?"

"Of sorts."

"Oh that's terrible." She said, his heart plummeted, he was right he shouldn't be around her. Even she was disagreeing with his company now. He wished he had kept his mouth shut. She was no doubt going to tell him how barbaric fighting was and that he was a cruel barbarian for being in such battles. "You must be so traumatised by what you have seen."

He stopped. Literally stopped dead in his tracks. Did he detect compassion in her voice? He looked down at her face and her eyebrows were furrowed, her lips ever so slightly parted. She looked upset just looking at him. What did she mean? "I do not understand you." He told her honestly.

"War must be a horrible thing to witness; I bet you still see it when you sleep." That he did. "I bet what you have seen and been forced to do has shaped you forever. Is that why you can not dance or start conversation? Have you not been long in our society?"

"... It is getting late I am sure you are not allowed to be out for so long. Let us find you a pretty ribbon or trinket for you to take home with you."

Her hand was still in the crook of his arm, he turned away from her again and started walking down the street, forcing her to continue walking as well. What on earth was he supposed to say to that?

"This is the shop. I have been coming here since I was a little girl." She said as they opened the door and the brass bell chimed loudly in their ears announcing their presence. She made no other remarks about his army life and carried on as if that conversation had never taken place. He was intensely grateful to her for that, he compassion made him uncomfortable. He had never had that sort of attention before.

She walked over to a square table laid out with various samples of coloured ribbon. Some with frills and some with bows. Many were plain but dyed lilacs and pinks, reds and yellows; feminine colours for female decoration. He looked at the 'fluff' on the table and wondered what it was women wanted with such random strips of material. He hadn't been around many women and the one woman he knew well was Lily who rarely wore 'ribbon'.

"You have never been in one of these shops?"

"No."

"Well see this lilac one? I want to wrap it around the rim of my hat to make it prettier but those thin strips I will use to tie my hair up at night so in the morning I have these tight curls."

"You hair isn't naturally like that?"

"Like this? Oh no, these curls are too small to be natural. My mama helps me braid and wind my hair at night and then I sleep with it all funny. Every morning I unwind my hair and it's curly. Then it's styled."

"Oh."

"I take it you have no brothers or sisters."

"I had a sister once; she did not make it past childhood."

"Oh I'm sorry."

"What's done is done."

She pondered over another few pieces of material before finally choosing some and paying. That would entertain her mother for a while and be a useful prop to her father inquisitive questions on where she had been that day.

"I have to get back soon but will you escort me half way?"

"Of course."

Her hand once more in the crook of his arm they left. She hoped the shop keeper did not mention anything about seeing her in the shop with a strange man. Her mother would have a fit. At that thought she prayed that no one at all, that knew her, would see her walking down the streets with a man. She would have no reputation left at all if she were to be seen. Joseph noticed her restlessness and nudged her slightly, "I know of a another way back that is less populated."

"May we take it, we should really be chaperoned."

"Yes, follow me."

He took her out of sight of the populated town and down a little alley that if followed would lead toward a field. He Took her down the path and then asked where it was she needed to get to. She promptly told him and he led her onwards. Taking advantage of her had never been on his mind but he was aware of how easy that would be if he was a decent man. "You are foolish to come down such secluded places with a stranger."

"Are you going to hurt me?"

"No, but that isn't the point. The point is anyone could hurt you and I don't want you repeating this act with anyone but me or your father."

"Understood, Sir." She taunted a little. "So what's the hottest country you've been to?"

"I've been to many countries. I've travelled most of Africa, that's the hottest continent I've been to."

"That must be simply amazing! Tell me of it."

What could he say? He had fought a bloody battle in the desert. The cold wind had whipped at his face, the sand had clung to his hair. It gripped the roots and made it so that it had taken a week of constant washing to get it out. He knew that during the day the desert heat would kill him in minutes and every day at the dawn there was a rush to flee both enemy and sun. It was a race he hoped never to repeat in his life. That was the most dangerous part. The part they all feared the most. As for the sights and spenders of the country he had seen very few. The pyramids of Egypt of course he had seen once, but it was but a fleeting visit. The tombs of kings he had spent time in but it took a lot if effort to recall memories from so long ago. A time of fear and battle and war cries. The screaming from those days haunted his ears even as he thought of it. The sand he had felt scratching at his skin was a reminder that his life was but a dull pain. Always to be felt never to escape. The loneliness and battle would never leave him, like the sand that clung to his hair with a death like grip.

"Most of what I saw was battle. The deserts are bitterly cold in the night but I know the heat during the day is almost unbearable."

He recalled the dawn he didn't quite made it in time. The ten minutes he spent running in the desert as the sun slowly rose and burned him. Killing him. Ten minutes and he was in shelter; collapsing and screaming in agony for water. For the magic of vampires to cool his blistered and scorched skin.

"The war was brutal, we almost did not win."

He had won by the skin of his teeth and it took two months to recover. Two months of strangers tending to him because he couldn't walk, couldn't feed but was classed as one of the best soldiers around simply because he was strong enough to survive. The ground had been littered with bodies when he was pulled free by fellow kin.

"I saw the valley of the kings however. It was dark, but our tour guide had lights. The sun had not completely set. The road in the desert was winding and the tombs themselves were... extraordinary. We entered one and it was a corridor of sorts leading towards the actual tomb, the casket was enclosed and in the middle of the room and all around painted on the walls were various pictures. Three types of snake were drawn on the walls. I remember one; vertical it was and faded in colour because of how long it had been on there. The walls, they were a faint hue of yellow. The pictures however were in reds and greens and blues. Brightly coloured. It must have been nothing less than a masterpiece when it was first created. Still is."

"It sounds wonderful."

"It was."

It had been the reward for surviving. He had recovered and insisted he see something to take his mind of the images of war and fallen comrades. His healer had smiled and led him from his room out into the desert and given him a tour. It had been a good end to a terrible stay. The conversation once again dwindled out but he felt happy in her company. He didn't feel the need to talk and she actually had a smile on her face as he walked her back.

This happy moment would be just like the tour through the tombs. It would be nice while it was happening but gone very quickly. He had to go, he had to leave her, and he had to go back to war.

"Will you meet again tomorrow? I can tell my father I need another basket or hat or something of the sort."

"Yes." Was his reply. "The same time?"

"That would be fine."

He left her when he saw her veering off towards a stately home. He had already agreed to see her again. A part of him knew that he would regret staying with her for so long; it would make leaving her so hard to do. But a part of him was determined to see her as much as possible before his time was up and he had no choice but to leave.

"Good night Joseph." She said lightly letting go of his arm and walking away.

He felt a wrenching in his chest as he watched her walk off. He had a desperate urge to tell Perttu of all that had happened. He wanted to share his interesting hour with his brother and speak about how he felt. He thought better of it though and hurried away; the night was young and he wanted to walk in the refreshing darkness for a while.

Chapter 3

Tomorrow dawned and tomorrow faded. He had not met her instead he had woken, paced the floor and watched the time tick down until such time when he could say, "I stood her up." Never before did he think the words would represent himself – such a dishonour was it to break his word. And the offense went further; he had left a woman alone on the streets, unaccompanied. That was low. To purposely allow a woman to be in danger, to him and his upbringing, was nothing less than criminal. He tried telling himself he had meant to go but lost track of time but that was a lie. He had meant not to go.

Going meant attachment. It meant being so intrigued that he got caught up in the affairs of mortals and he was too dark to put them in danger and risk his own mentality. Therefore, in short, Joseph - the elite, cold and indifferent soldier - was a coward. Which served only to remind him that he needed to go. He had no choice but to leave. Whatever it was that made it so he was drawn to this mortal woman wasn't good enough to stop him doing his duty. That was his sole purpose to life; or so he had been brought up to understand.

From the corner of the estate he watched as the candle-lit rooms of the house were plunged, one by one, into darkness until the outline of the house were all most people would see. A half hour of standing and watching the windows in case he managed to catch a tiny glimpse of her had come to nothing. He had not seen her. He did not even know which room she lay asleep in. But he couldn't leave without seeing her one last time.

With his left hand clasping tightly a small gift he made his way over to the house. It was but a small thing to undo the lock. A mere touch on the lock had it undoing thanks to his trained magic. For once he liked being what he was. The familiar snick sounded and he pushed open the front door. A modest house greeted him, with mismatching fabrics and bright primary colours. It looked to be decorated by many people all at once, eccentric people at that. It didn't seem to fit his elegant woman and yet at the same time it suited her. It tied in well with the laughter that always seemed to be playing on her face and the light mood in which she took everything about him, even when he had refused to dance with her that very first night.

Still décor as bold as this was certainly not what he was used to. When he stayed at his own home it was stark. Bare walls and minimal furniture adorned his dwelling and only as he took in the blue and yellow flowers did he crave a woman. For the first time he wanted his dull and practical house to feel the warmth of a woman's touch. He wouldn't mind if those silly throws were placed over the top of a couch. He found himself anticipating the moment when Elsa would ask him to go shopping for matching plates and tea cups complete with saucers. It was a sure sign of his weakness and so he hurried through the house.

He was a soldier on demand for a reason. Silently he prowled the corridors of the house, ignoring the lower floors as he knew there were no bedrooms there. Instead he took the stairs. With bent knees and light footsteps... and a little well controlled magic, he took each step silently. Nothing could be heard in the almost silent house. He heard the people breathing, the sheets rustling and somewhere was the licking tongue of a dog asleep but he suspected the animals was lower down in the kitchen.

The bedrooms were not locked and that only made it much easier for him to open each door and peer inside but many rooms where empty. One held a female, a beautiful, black haired female who slept facing the door with her eyes shut in peace and a tiny smile etched onto her face. Another held a man, a young one, just past sixteen he bet. The stern features were already a part of the young ones face and the sandy blonde hair still held a visible line from a middle parting. A rich boy. Obvious in this kind of family home but the look hadn't faded even in sleep.

Joseph was getting frustrated by the time he found her. He had even found her parents before he found her she was in off to the rooms furthest away from all the others. He didn't know if that was a good thing or not. They wouldn't hear her if anything was wrong and yet it meant he had more privacy with her. It was a seesaw of equal pro and con. Once he found her he wasted no time in walking into her bedroom and closing the door behind him.

She slept with her hair twisted by strips of ribbon. For curls she had told him and now he understood why she bought ribbon. It looked painful though; the ribbon was tight around hair and it couldn't be comfortable for her to sleep with. Still her face was free from emotion, it was relaxed and soft. A white gown hung from her and her blankets were pulled up to her chest to keep off the draft, her tiny hands still held onto the edge of the beige covers. No doubt she had fallen asleep still holding them over her.

He didn't like to see her holding onto them so he reached over and pulled the blankets further up to her chin patting them around to make sure they clung around her and hugged her to keep in the warmth. He didn't want her getting ill. Her lips were pressed together as she slept; his vampiric eyesight letting him see such a beautiful colour. Delicate cherry red lips on healthy skin made his mouth water. He desired her not just as a man but as something more. Something he still wasn't understanding.

Fear crossed his mind. He wondered if his body was seeing her a potential source of food; he feared that he was acting like a predator at that moment when all he really wanted to do was stroke back her brown locks of hair so he could see her rosy cheek even better. He wanted to run his knuckles over her skin just to see if it felt as soft as it looked. Having pressed the blankets around her tightly he was hyper aware of her figure. No large skirt was there now to keep him away from her, nor hide the delicious curves of a female body.

Lust was a strong force in him and he didn't like it. He wanted to know more than just her body but she was asleep and he didn't want her to wake and see him either. It would terrify her to think he had broken into her house, and so easily as well. He was ashamed that he had not met her that night to spend precious hours with her and get to know this Elsa.

The gift in his hand was a single rose. It was all he could give her at the moment as he had left his house for war and not for a woman. He had needed no food nor clothes and had brought no money with him, though, he was rich back at home. The thorns had been removed from the dull green stem and the vivid blood red blossom was even an even darker shade than her lips. Placing it on her bedside table the logic kicked in anyway; she would know he had been in her house, her very bedroom. She would wake to his gift and most likely think only the worst of him. Think him a threat to her.

He sighed, it wasn't how he wanted her to remember him but at the same time he would not leave her without trying to woo her, even just a little. He had gone past his own logic at this point, he wouldn't be coming back so let he was letting himself go through with this stupidity. He let himself lay it gently on the sanded wood and take a piece of paper that was on her desk. Taking the quill in his hand he wrote her a little note,

Elsa,

When you wake I will have gone. My sincerest apologies for breaking my word to you. I did not meet you as I said I would. Forgive me. Here is a rose as a token of my affection and sign of my apology.

Yours,

Jospeh.

That was all he could do. So he placed the paper next to the rose and looked one last time at the only woman he had ever shown any interest in.

Her deep breathing was rhythmic, paced and he found himself trying to match it. His own breathing slowed, coming in slower yet fuller. He felt his shoulder relax until he was no longer tense. She was already doing wonders for him.

"I'm sorry that I can not stay with you." He whispered to her.

Enough was enough and he turned away heading back to the door to leave her to her rest.

"Joseph?" Spinning around he saw Elsa's eyes open, staring at him. "Is this a dream?" she asked.

"Yes, it's all a dream. Go back to sleep."

"You didn't meet me today."

"I'm sorry Elsa."

"My father was angry I stayed out so late. I waited for you. It got too cold, I had to come home."

"It won't happen again."

"It had best not."

Even her voice, which was groggy and slurred slightly by sleep, managed to be light hearted. She accepted his words so quickly and wasn't angry with him. It made his heart clench.

"I have to go." He said, his voice breaking a little at the end. He couldn't explain why it did; he was just suddenly overcome with emotion at the thought of leaving her. "Wait for my return." He mumbled before slipping out of the door; not even waiting for a reply. He shook his head and cursed silently. He couldn't believe he had once again made a commitment to her!

Chapter 4

Almost late he had ran hard to get to the battle he was needed at. A battle between two sets of vampires was not all that common anymore. Not since the 'white days' anyway. But still they occurred. When he was almost at the south of England, coming up to the battlefield that the moon lit up for him, he wondered to himself whether he had ran 'to' the battle or 'from' Elsa. He had ran like hounds were snapping at his ankles.

He had been greeted like a brother. His arms clasped in a tight hold that told a little too much about the people he was fighting alongside. Their fingers had dug in and gripped his arm in a sign of desperation and sincere relief that he had come to aid them. Time was dwindling and as the commander of one unit was guiding him through the ranks of preparing vampires and explaining the details to him, Joseph was undergoing the change.

Letting go of the human illusion of himself he allowed his fangs to lengthen and sharpen to a point. His fingernails and toenails followed suit, followed by every hair on his body so his very skin was littered with blades. His body; thin, muscular with discretion and wiry, seemed to grow a little and his hair fell to the middle of his back, glinting in the moonlight like shiny metal. His animalistic nature crept out of him while at the same time he was listening intently to what had happened and what was going to follow. That had been on night one. They were now two nights into the battle and his appearance was still that of a murderous animal, the human form seemingly forgotten.

The ground was streaked with lines of red. Blood red. A dark colour that was thick as it coated the dirt on the ground. The little pebbles and grit that made up the battleground stuck to the thickened liquid that was drying only too quickly and becoming a sticky substance. It wasn't nice to look at and it wasn't nice to walk on. In. It slicked the soles of his feet and where it hadn't yet started to dry it sprayed softly as he took his steps. The oozing mess leaving patter stains on the backs of his calves. He had travelled with only the clothes on his back and he was glad he had taken them off before the battle. He looked forward to the bathe in the nearest river that he would take after the battle and he looked forward to putting back on human clothes. When he saw Elsa again he would be handsome again and clean, hopefully that way she would not be ashamed to be seen with him as she no doubt would be if she were to see his body now - coated with thick hair and a gory mess that wasn't even his.

That mere fact that a woman was plaguing his mind during the midst of a battle was a sign that she had edged too far into his life. Another annoying voice in his head was telling him it was a sign that he was ready to put aside this life of his and start afresh. His stomach lurched with the thought of a better life, one that included the fairer sex who could teach him the meaning of gentleness and maybe even laughter; as she seemed accustomed to doing.

Two days into war and the sounds of slaughter were so common he no longer heard them for what they were. They drowned out most conversation between his own side but in general he couldn't make out which were cries of anger and which were pain. And which was saddened grief at the loss of a friend. He stopped telling which noises came from friend or foe after little over a day and he found he didn't want to know. His fallen brethren he would no doubt see at the end and that would be the time to mourn them. To weep and fall to the floor for them. Not that he would weep, he was trained not to weep but he would kneel in honour for them though.

The tiny fine hairs that coated his skin were now on edge, little blades of their own ready to slice into anything that dared to touch him. Keeping his arms crossed over his chest making the sign of an 'X' he was fully ready to defend himself and even attack but his skill lay not in the actual fight, but in the tactics of stealth.

Years and years of battle had allowed Joseph to phase out that sounds of war, as background noise it kept his mind from going fuzzy. His feet were walking over the blood covered floor instead of standing his ground and fighting because he was eager to get somewhere. He needed to find the enemy's weakness. Then he would use his sorcerer's magic. He loved that somewhere in ancient history the vampire race had intermingled (if only for a short while) with the sorcerers. Now the lethal feline predator that was a vampire had the added defence/offence of sorcerer's magic. Not as good of course, he loved to watch Niklas using his magic, for sorcerers always wielded such power much better and with a hint more grace than a vampires did. And Niklas his friend, had very quickly learnt to become a master even over others of his own race.

This battle was almost over; two days of fighting, scouting and defending and Joseph had finally found the perfect spot and was almost at it. The ones at the back of the battlefield were young, inexperienced and foolish to the point of exasperation. They were lazy joining in on the battle only when it suited them and caused them the most amusement. They had a distinct lack of discipline and for a while Joseph had ignored simply because he had thought them children, brought along for 'experience' only. Until he had understood, their foolishness was a distraction; creeping out around them was a force - a whisper of disturbed air.

Like a flammable gas or liquid the air around them was designed to blow up and they were pushing that 'air' forward, throughout the whole of the warriors with the aim of focusing it on one side and then... boom. What he didn't particularly like about this very sophisticated and sneaky tactic was it was to go boom on his side. He didn't feel like flying through the air in twenty different pieces so he was currently employing a nice magical technique of his own. One of a shield. He wasn't called to battle for nothing. An army doesn't fight without a shield of sorts and Joseph was very good at his vampire magic.

Using magic took a lot of concentration and energy for the new ones, decades (maybe even a century, he was no longer sure) that concentration became second nature. The feeling was the same; it felt like he was pushing something out of his very pores. He inched his way around the mass of soldiers that were all running at each other and tearing at each other's skin with the hairs of their body. Like windmills certain soldiers moved their hair, a very soft clicking sound to be heard as the sharpened and pointed ends clicked together, knives in their own right.

Perttu walked with a bend in his knees and hunch to his back. It was a crawl akin to a cat inching around. It allowed him to go unnoticed, making his way around and behind vampire and rocks with ease, his eyes piercing his surroundings making sure he wasn't caught, making sure they didn't see him. His hearing was letting the blur of background screams lull him into a hypnotic sense. A war trance while at the same time listening out for sounds a little closer to hand. Nothing had spotted him; no one was going to stop him. This war between two sets of vampires was horrifically saddening. No brethren should fight each other but at the same time he knew for what he fought for. He knew the side he belonged to. He picked his battles wisely, with purpose, in the past even choosing the right side knowing his life was forfeit. Weird how that forfeit had still not killed him.

With his fangs out ready to pounce he closed his eyes for a millisecond. This life was not the life he wanted anymore. A young man was crouched infront of him, 'young' was a term he used judging by the vague look in his face. The vampiric nature had however taken the little humanity he may have had from his features and replaced it with an angry merciless and cold expression, just as it had with Joseph. The man was blind to all but his own laughter at the blood - crazed with the sight of gluttonous feasting he had crouched in preparation of tasting that river of blood. Joseph lunged.

His teeth three inches long but he used his forearm to pin the man at the neck. The hairs on his body dug into the flesh of his neck, dug in and sank deep holding him still like teeth locking. Joseph's naked body fell onto the half clothed man; his whole body coated in hair was now a whole body full of piercing blades that anchored his enemy to the floor. His fangs buried themselves deep into his enemy's neck; into the pulsating veins and arteries that lay but millimetres under the tender flesh.

Joseph gulped. Gulped in fluid and nutrients. A bonus to a vampire was that they could sustain themselves even in battles – feeding off their kills. The downside meant that vampire wars could last for years without ever stopping, there was no need to if no one needed to replenish their strength. The man he had pinned was responsible for the soon to be bomb and as Joseph gulped the man's blood he felt him weaken, his power dulling, fading with each gulp Joseph took. So he latched onto the power, using the blood as an aid to 'feel' the very essence of the enemy under him. Feeding gave the chance and he took control of that power. Just as the man's eyes closed in death Joseph snatched from him that line of magic; the bomb was now in his control.

Wasting no more time he pulled it back, pulled it away from his own side further towards the back were there were only the enemy and striving to keep it away from the middle where a terrible mix of both his 'brothers' and his enemy battled. Once the flammable energy was pulled back, thrown to the far end, he started to let it go, igniting the energy that had been let loose. Wrenching his fangs from the man he smirked, "time to fly."

Letting go of the magic he saw the yellow spark and the flicker of orange until a burst of violent flames erupted feet from him and evolved into a ball of fire. Like the sun it burned bright, like an orb, and the flames licked at those all around for feet. The force from that initial burst of flames had sent Joseph flying backwards into the air. Though untouched by the wicked flames he still had to expect a painful landing but it was this part he loved.

With his skin prickling, then tickling softly the feeling of cold water trickling down in rivulets on a hot summers evening took over his body. And he let it, encouraged it. Forced it as he manipulated his own magic. The relief this feeling induced caused a slight relaxation to his muscles which allowed his body to seem limp: perfect for a landing. But the feeling on his skin was his own magic, it was his shield. Wrapping around his body was a cushion of air, a padding which mixed with his own relaxation meant that the flight he experienced felt a lot slower. It felt like a full minute of bliss. It was as though there was a tiny pause in the battle where he was allowed to regain himself and breath properly.

His body hit the ground, ass first the heels. His shoulder blades followed by shoulders bumped to the muddy ground and the back of his head just lightly tapped to a stop before the rest of his body made contact. And then he burst out laughing.

"Day two!" He cried out. "And we have won." Elsa I'm coming to court you. The latter was spoken softly in his mind while the rest of the enemy either fled, surrendered or finished fighting to the death for a shred of honour to be left in their names.

Chapter 5

The noise of battle died down, the snarling and spiting and gulping of blood all died down. Joseph, who was laid on the floor, took a look around. The high he had just experienced as he had won them their battle suddenly disappeared as he took a look around him.

The ground was scorched from the bomb. The remains of vampires lay scattered everywhere, their bloodied dismembered limbs and bodies flung everywhere. Their faces in death lost their animalistic sheen to be replaced with the human face of one who could be mistaken as asleep. Until you saw the wounds that is. Their pale faces covered were in tiny scraps and scratches, their necks held the marks of fangs. Trails of blood ran down the skin of the dead and the whole seen looked barbaric, vicious. Pure hellish.

The stench finally hit his nose. Two days, or well nights to the humans, had been so hectic he had barely given much thought to the familiar smell but now it clogged his nose and made him want to gag. The heavy smell of blood clung to the air where it dried and putrefied on the ground and it was disgusting. He coughed a little and stood up. The smell of sweat hung around everyone, they had not washed, instead they had fought to such an extent that sweat beads still clung to their foreheads. And now in the dirty battleground the stale, sickly, salty smell started to burn his nose. He could smell it even on himself. His eyes went back to normal, his fangs shrank. The hair on his body lay flat once more and he looked at his very skin. His bare feet should have been muddy from walking on the ground but instead they were coated with blood, dried blood that was thick and sticky on him. It would not come off easily. And the splashes on the backs on his calves – they also travelled around to the front. His legs were covered in the blood of the dead that lay around him and he suspected that his back and hair would also be covered in it as well having just fallen backwards on to it.

He felt repulsed at his own appearance and then the damage he had inflicted on his own kin; the vampires that had attacked him. Brothers in a sense, they shared some genetic makeup. They to had fought for a cause they felt strongly about, just like him. Usually he felt nothing after battle, usually he turned and walked away leaving his 'side' to clear the fields while he merely cleaned up and showed up for the honour funeral before leaving to go to another battle.

He didn't know what exactly changed, all he knew was that for the first time he wanted to be anywhere other than the battle, he was struggling to even remain composed for a minute, let alone the hours it would take for the funerals to begin. He wanted to go back to Elsa but the thought of her in her clean dress and her infectious laughter only shamed him more as he thought of his shaming state in comparison.

"Joseph, thank you for your aid. It is thanks to you that we won this battle."

"You are most welcome."

He relayed his rehearsed speech, the one he always said so they did not feel bad about asking for his help. Usually he didn't mind, he had known no other life than fighting for others, now however he did mind. Now he wanted to get away and never be asked again.

"You know you are needed on the east coast two weeks from now. There is to be another battle and our kin there are sorely under soldiered. We are travelling there in three days' time to join them if you wish to accompany us."

"No I have business elsewhere I must attend to. Thank you for your offer though."

Dragging him to war was not his idea of thanks at that moment.

"You will be there though, Joseph?"

"Of course I will be there. I promised their leader I would be, many weeks back. I do not go back on my word."

"Then we shall fight alongside one another again Joseph. I look forward to it." The commander held out a blood stained hand for Joseph to take and shake. He did so, ignoring the lump in his throat that he felt as his own slick hand slid a little in the grip of the commander. Why had he promised to go to another war? Why had he once again signed away his fate? His time with Elsa would be cut short, his disgust would deepen and his own appearance would once again be unfit for such presence of a woman. He closed his eyes. He couldn't simply walk away from this. He was trained to be the best and battles were lost simply because he wasn't there. He hated now his own skill. His own strength had condemned and cursed him. He wanted to see what society felt like, what it tasted like. What it was to sit down with a woman and let them wipe away all traces of brutality and make him feel... 'clean' again.

The commander walked away leaving Joseph to his thoughts. Damn it all. He looked back at the slowly burning trees and the naked vampires walking amongst the fallen picking out their friends and carrying them to the side. He couldn't stay there a minute longer. He ran from the battlefield. His feet sliding a little with the coating of blood he had on them making him slip. He pushed his legs to a burn he went that fast. His nose was sniffing, searching. He wanted water. He wanted soap. He wanted to be clean. He smelt only his own stench as panic settled in his heart. Would he ever be clean again? Would he ever smell clean and look clean because if he didn't there would be no going back to Elsa.

His frantic searching took him deep into woods and his ears were so filled with his own horrible thoughts he didn't notice the sound of a stream. He didn't notice the smell of fresh water or the taste of purity in the air. He was blind to the water until he fell into it. His feet running off the bank did not find purchase until his head was submerged and his feet grazed across the sandy bottom of the small stream.

His heart calmed at once. His breathing eased back to normal and his frantic thoughts slowed down as he realised the water around him was red. He was being washed the blood, his sins almost, being washed away by the calming, cool water. He came up spitting and dragging in huge amounts of air.

"It isn't every day a bloody soldier comes and disturbs my home."

"Wha-!"

Whipping around Joseph turned to see the most extraordinary creature stood before him. A woman he was sure of that, with golden hair that hung down in waves to her waist. She was dressed all in white, but it was a simple dress with white girdle and a white cloak over her dainty shoulders. She looked beautiful, slender and tall she was middle-aged but aging well. Her face was neither in a smile nor in a frown and her words hadn't sounded angry. He was captivated by the look of her, puzzled that one such as her was in such s as a forest, she should be in a palace for sure. What made him wonder at her species was a faint golden light that seemed to hover around his whole aura. He couldn't understand why he saw her aura, not many creatures in the entire world could perceive someone aura and he was not one of them. He shouldn't be seeing it which meant she was something special.

"Not many men have managed to stand so still when they look at me. Men have fallen to their knees, others have tried to approach me. You do neither. You do not look at me with lust; you look at me with confusion. You are a strange one."

At that he almost laughed. Him strange when a woman lived in the forest and looked like an angel. "I think it is you who is the strange one." He chuckled lightly. She smiled at him then, a whisper of emotion that she quickly hid.

"What brings you here, barbarian?" He winced at that.

"Running from the battlefield on which I fought for my people."

He didn't mean to chastise her but he wanted her to know he did not fight for himself.

"You think I do not see you." She suddenly demanded. "You chose your battle according to your beliefs, you fight in them because you know no other way of life. It not for your people that you do this."

"I do not fight without thought."

"That you don't but still you fight. Why not use the brains you were gifted with and think of diplomacy instead of war."

"Because vampires can not talk to each other without getting angry or without arguing and then fighting."

"Ah, the White days have taken their toll on you. Well come Soldier, clean yourself and tell me of this lady you are thinking about. I invite you to dine with me."

She stood up from the rock she was reclined on and looked at him. He blushed when he saw that he was naked in her presence but found that he was clean. Every inch of him was pale white skin, no blood splashes, no lingering spots that clung under his fingernails or in the creases of his skin. He was clean as if he had been scrubbing at himself for hours. As he looked back at her for an explanation she inclined her head a little.

"You were uncomfortable, bloodied as you were, I thought I would make you feel better. Refresh yourself in my pool though; the water will help to relax your muscles. As you can see, the water is no longer red."

It wasn't. What magic was this? This was no harsh sorcerer's magic, it did not hold the rough masculine sensation that sorcerer's magic did. This was woven, graceful and beautiful. He didn't understand but the whole surroundings seemed light and pure.

"I sense your confusion but do not fear. You know only sorcerers and vampires who wield magic. I am an enchantress. And I wield a different sort of magic. One that does not fit in with the warring of other kinds."

He turned to follow her instructions and submerge himself in the water again but her soft voice called back to him – with a hint of amusement – "hurry up Joseph, Elsa is waiting for you and her father want's her married before her birthday."

Chapter 6

"Joseph, have you ever worn a suit?"

"What? Yes of course I have."

"Have you ever been comfortable in such attire?"

He followed this beautiful woman as she led him through the wonderful landscape. His bare feet walked upon water-smoothed pebbles and all around him was lush greenery that looked more healthy than a plump newborn. "I can't say that I have to be honest. The collars choke me."

"Interesting. Then I will have to custom make your new suit."

"What?!"

He grumbled. He didn't want a suit and didn't really understand what she was saying.

"Do you live here?" He asked.

"I dwell here, yes."

"On your own?"

"I prefer the solitude. I have gifts I do not want to burden others with."

"Oh."

He wasn't a man of words so he simply stayed silent at the end of that sentence. He looked down at his attire. Fighting naked meant that he had no clothing on him so this woman had provided him with some. A simple open shirt and trousers covered him. He didn't mind this shirt, though he preferred the tunics he usually wore when he was not fighting or courting women from high society. His tunics were loose fitted and open for about two inches at the neck. He detested shirts ironed until stiff and buttoned until it lay on the base of his throat and irritated him.

The sleeves of his tunics held tight to his arm, moving with him and not getting in his way. Shirt sleeves always dangled and were baggy and got caught on everything that was around. They were cumbersome. "I already have an idea for a shirt for you."

"I don't want to wear a shirt."

"You will have to."

"Why?"

He wasn't wearing one of those things unless he was going to be in human society again. He didn't like them. He didn't see what she was talking about.

"Don't act like a child, accept it and deal with it." Came the reply to his question. He scowled.

"I don't like baggy clothes. It isn't practical. They get in the way of everything and imagine if I was attacked, I would have to brush them out of my way before I can defend myself."

"Always on alert." She mumbled under her breath dipping low to avoid a low hanging branch. Stuck in his bitter moaning Joseph didn't see the branch and face palmed it. "Besides Joseph, do you want to impress that lovely lady? I'm sure I can create something for you that would be simply breath-taking for her to see you in."

His ears perked up. "Such as?"

"I'm thinking, you'll see when I have the design fully worked out. Now then do you want to eat?" Infront of them was a long wooden table laid with lots and lots of food. It literally overflowed with meats and cheeses. Wine was held in a clear pitcher in the middle of the table and tall crystal glasses with long stems to hold were lined all around the table.

"How many are dinning here?"

"I said that I dwelt here alone but I do have guests at times. My kin have come to greet you today."

"Me?"

"Yes. There was a council not long ago. We desired a solution and you were the name that ended our debate."

"You've lost me."

"Then pour yourself a glass of wine and drink it. The rest will be joining us shortly."

Again and again she pulled the brush through her waist length hair. She was to have breakfast with her father but she didn't want to go downstairs. She had heard from a servant what had happened the night before and she knew the pressure would now be put upon her twicefold. She wanted to go about her day seeing her friends and congratulating her best friend on such a happy occasion. Instead she would be greeting strange men and having to watch her manners, her posture and her tongue as she was expected to take tea with every one of them and try to find a suitable husband.

She was tiring of life. She found herself looking at her maid with envy. Yes her maid worked hard but her face wasn't just lined with hard work it was lined with laughter. Laugh lines around her mouth and at the corners of her eyes defined her maid's old but feminine face.

"Was you married Sasha?" She asked.

"Oh once, a long time ago. It ended a little too suddenly for my liking though."

"What happened? If you don't mind me asking?"

The maid paused in her duties, letting the bedspread fall in disarray on the bed. The tidying seemed to be forgotten as the older lady looked at Elsa.

"Why do you ask dear, you have always been kind to us, always conversed with us dear but you have never asked the personal questions."

"I just want to know what is so different from your life and mine."

Shrewd eyes stared into Elsa's and she felt rather intimidated for a minute.

"I was young and it was my night off from work. I had waited a long time for this night but I was going to a dance with some of my friends. I met Luke there. We danced and agreed to meet for a drink on my next day off. I have always been a servant but when we decided to marry I put my notice in with my last employer and together we started up a home. I was pregnant within the year. He was called to war after that and sadly he died within six months of his going away. I was alone to raise the child, a little boy I called Smithy. I had nothing, I could not find work. I had friends that tried to help me but when Smithy got ill I couldn't afford the medicine. He died as well and I was left to find employment. And here I am. I have been here twenty years now."

"I'm so sorry Sasha, I didn't know. I wouldn't have asked you to tell me such a painful story if I had known."

She was shocked, so terribly sad for this woman who had lost those she loved most dearly.

"Do not look at me like that. I was depressed for a year after that but then I knew that I had no choice but to go on in the world. I have learnt to remember the good times instead. My Luke always made me laugh and I loved him dearly. I chose to marry him and we danced all the time. I do not regret anything. My little boy is with his father now."

"My father is trying to get me to marry. He has set up suitors for me to greet and I must choose one before my birthday. I only have six weeks."

"I have to say Miss Elsa that is one thing I do not envy you with. I fell in love with Luke, you are to be matched with someone you do not love."

"My father is only interested in getting me out of the house so it is one less worry for him."

"He worries you will never marry and will have no support when he is gone. He does not want to see you on the streets with nothing to your name."

"That is not true, you know it is not. He worries only that his money is going to some well-connected family and that a family tie can be sought and his business will get better. He does not worry about me. That is what other fathers do. Not mine."

The look on Sasha's face told Elsa that she had guessed correct. Sasha may only be a servant but she saw things others didn't. Heard things no one else did because everyone treated the servants as if they weren't alive let alone in the same room as the rich. So the servants knew a lot. It was painful to know her own father was going to pawn her off to some man just so his business would get bigger. It hurt to know that.

"Come on Miss, let us get you dressed, you cannot greet these fine men in your nightgown."

She could only hope to get an amiable man that would look after her in this match. There would be no love because she had already fallen in love. With Joseph. She didn't like that he was gone. That he had been gone a few days now. She had dreamt about that night she had gone to bed after he hadn't met her and woken up to a letter and rose. That was weird because she wondered if it was a dream or not and it was worse because she couldn't remember it. She had been far too sleepy to remember him if he had gotten into her house. Had he broken into her house then? Should she be scared of him? How had he managed it anyway, if indeed he had? Questions about Joseph ran around in her head everyday and all day. His letter had seemed to hold a finality to it that shook her to the core. She hated that he said that he would be gone. She wanted the chance to court him, maybe even marry him. She was sure her father would approve as he looked rich enough but then again if her father didn't know him then he might not.

The night before Mark had finally gotten the courage to ask Camilla for her hand in marriage and she had given it. It was a rare thing when one married for love around here but they were both rich children and would further both their parents business's so it was accepted and even celebrated. For some reason though this happy event just wouldn't leave her mind. She couldn't forsake the chance of her own happy ending. She wanted to remember Joseph's last words to her before he left that night – in her dreams or reality – but she couldn't. She found herself waiting for a man that she didn't know. It was hard. Harder still because even as she waited for him she had to be preparing for the other option: he might not come back. She had to flirt and get to know other men so if he did not come back to her she still had a chance to live a life.

It would be a life she wasn't happy with but what other choice did she have? She had nothing in this rich world. She was a woman; designed only to wait on her husband, run a household and provide children. To give up the money would be to have a chance at finding love but at the cost of severe hard work and a very reduced household and even food rations. She wouldn't be able to eat her favourite foods if she gave it up and her family would shun her. She would shame them and knock them down in the eyes of society. She couldn't be selfish and walk away, she couldn't not marry - that would burden her parents and then her youngest sister and brother as well when they married. She didn't know if she had the strength enough to leave everything and work as a servant anyway; to be always tired, always busy and getting hardly anything for the trouble.

She was stuck. Or so it felt. But that glimmer of light in the form of Joseph was still there, pondering on the sidelines it seemed. When would he return to her? She sank on the bed ignoring Sasha's rage at trying to get her into her chemise and moaning that she had just made that bed. Everything was forgotten. Her father had placed a strict time limit on this courting business. He wanted her gone by the end of six weeks. What if Joseph did not return in time and when he came back to her he found her married. She would forever hate herself for that. For not waiting long enough for him. But her father was not to be ignored.

Her kin as she called them soon arrived. Tall and slender men, a little on the feminine side themselves, walked over to the table and poured themselves glasses of wine holding them up to Joseph in salute before taking a sip. Women just as graceful, just as beautiful and just as glowing as the enchantress glided in and took their seats immediately. Glasses of wine were poured for them and they too toasted Joseph before sipping daintily from the crystal. Joseph was by now very puzzled.

"Don't look so guarded Joseph, it will all be explained. Well now we are here, let us eat."

Joseph was by nature a hard man. He looked the part, felt the part and no doubt sounded the part. He was wearing a white shirt courtesy of the enchantress but his wardrobe contained only black normally. His trousers themselves were black she had given him that little comfort at least. His hands were calloused and his very skin designed to cut someone to shreds with only a little thought on his part. His face was covered in a five o clock shadow that he was sure had already gotten a little bigger. Even his hair was a mess - made worse by washing and drying into a wavy, curling mess. And now he sat by women that looked so pure they were like glass and men that wore whites and silvers not only for shirts but for trousers also.

Everyone around this table looked graceful, dignified and quiet. They were soft spoken when they did speak and their hands looked so smooth he expected they would blister at the first sign of a sword. Joseph usually prized himself on his hard demeanour. He liked the command he wielded in the presence of anyone or anything. He enjoyed feeling as though he was always in control because he could always defend himself but at this table he was out of place. He the barbarian amongst the innocent and he didn't like it. He didn't feel in control it felt like he was an outsider. An outsider to be shunned and hated by such beautiful people.

So it surprised him when continually he was passed food and asked if he wanted a refill. He was shocked at the hands he shook and the smiles that were given to him in that graceful and concerned way. The men's blonde hair was straightened and long and flyaway and he half found himself wanted to feel it, just to feel the difference in his own wiry strands. He was slender himself, all vampires were but compared to them he looked rather muscly.

It was this constant comparison that had him wondering, what on earth was he doing here? What was the point and why were they looking at him as if he had made their dreams all come true.

"So Joseph where are you living these days?" The man closest to his right asked him.

"I don't really stay in one place. I own a house in the north of England but I rarely go there. I stay with my cousin at times. Sometimes anyway. He has lots of children. They like me to play with them but I don't think I'm good at it."

"Why is that?" He was a little shocked at the very personal question.

"I don't laugh." He said simply. "Children like laughter."

And it reminded him of what he couldn't have. The perfect family. Joseph was very happy with Lily. He had everything he could possible want and the children was the icing on top of the cake. Niklas was with them as an extra helping hand and Lily was content now. The children had a grandfather and grandmother there to be with them when their parents weren't and all in all it was a very happy family.

"Children like family Joseph. And they like it when people make the effort. Remember that when you go visiting next time."

The man on his right was rather blasé with his comment. It was as if a father was giving that little bit of fatherly advice while he was still taking a bite of his dinner. A simple irrelevant thought. "I'll bear it in mind."

"You don't close your shirts." One of the women commented.

"Sorry." He hastily went to close the buttons but another man on his left stopped him.

"Don't go worrying, she is just curious. Be who you want to be, especially amongst friends."

"Oh, well, ok. I don't usually wear shirts."

"Vampires fight naked don't you?" The same lady asked.

"Yes we do."

"Why?"

He was afraid that he would frighten her if he were to tell her. He could feel his temper raising with this peace. He felt like he was trying to be someone else. He felt he ought to be someone else in such pleasant company. It all felt a little forced.

"Yes we do. We are animals my lady. We cannot fight with clothes on - it would be pointless."

"Why?"

"Are you actually curious or are you mocking?"

That gained everyone's attention. "I am curious." Her genteel voice was not bothered by his demanding question. He praised her for her sturdy nerves.

"I am sorry. I am so different from you I thought you were mocking me." It was hard to describe so he placed down his fork and rolled back the sleeve of his shirt and held out his arm along the table towards her. "Do not touch, even if you want to. I would hurt you if you did and that is not my intention." He kept eye contact with her as he said that so she understood both the warning and the sincerity in his tone.

He let the façade drop, the humanity diminish but only in his arm, he could not do his entire body at the table. "As you can see the hairs stand up. They become like knives. They are our weapons. If I wore clothing over it," He pulled down his shirt and moved his arm a small amount, just enough to pass for everyday movement and the hair ripped the material. It was not clean rips either, the material frayed. On someone's skin it would decimate it. "It would ruin the clothes and the material would get in my way."

"Wow it's incredible. You're natural soldiers then." She commented.

"So it would seem. Yet, not all choose such a life. And those who do go through many a hardship. You can hold a sword but it does not mean you can wield it."

Silence greeted his words.

"And well said." The man to his right announced standing up with his glass in hand. "Which is why we chose you Joseph. You know the world better than any but we know diplomacy better than you. So we are going to ask that you dress the part, learn the words and then add your own little flare to things."

"What do you mean?"

"The wars of course. Don't tell me you haven't noticed, I know you have. The wars are increasing in this country. Over land and over kin and it is beginning to drag other species into a war between only one. We want you to stop the wars before they become like the White Days of old."

"I don't-;"

"It's simple Joseph, we want to show you another way to end the wars that doesn't mean you must strip off your clothes and coat yourself in blood. We are offering a chance to do what you were born to do, in a more humane way. We'll make a hero out of you as well. Do you accept the request?"

Chapter 7

Joseph shook his head. "I want to go back up north. I want to get to know Elsa."

"We are offering you retirement. This is a steadfast way of getting it."

"Retirement or death?"

"Either depending on how you handle the situation. You can still be with Elsa. There is time yet. We need to figure out exactly what is the underlying cause of this strange tension between you vampires. It is taking away our land Joseph. We need to live in the woods and forest of this world. Without our trees and streams and flowers we are nothing. We are hidden Joseph and we do not do well exposed. Your race is tearing up the ground and pushing us further away from each other and we are left to roam for land. The hounds are restless wanting your noise to stop so they can live in solitude that your cousin Perttu pushed onto them. You have sorcerers who try to pick a winning side so they might further their own power and you have young vampires born into a quarrel that is not their own but are forced to participate in none the less. Amongst your own race Joseph these wars are pushing you all to kill the innocent."

It was true, he knew it was. He had seen the worse wars known in their history and he knew the consequences such extreme conditions had on everyone and everything in close contact.

"I know what war does."

"Then you must understand why we want to end it."

"I cannot walk over to battling vampires dressed in a suit and demand they put down their weapons."

"No you cannot; but you can go infront of fighting vampires dressed with dignity and composure and shock them into a split second pause. That pause will gain you an advantage only you Joseph can wield. Or do you think we do not know how you hold back on your power?"

"I hold nothing back."

"You lie!" The enchantress suddenly stood up. Her eye flashed anger, "We have watched you a while now Joseph, we have heard about you. The White Days took such a toll on you that it was not only a miracle you survived but it changed you... physically and mentally. The warring you had no choice but to live through developed your skills. You are a master at war Joseph and though you do not want it and hide it as much as you can while still winning for your side, you are thrice the man you show the world!"

The food did not look so good anymore. It tasted a little bitter in his mouth. He didn't want to talk about the White Days, it made him feel sick. He especially wasn't in the mood to talk about his abilities either. It was bad enough that he hid them from Perttu.

"Joseph." A woman came from the top of the table over to him grabbing his hand as she looked into his eyes. "We chose you, not to torment you and hurt you as you think but because we know you are the right man for this very tough decision. Your skill was not meant to be hidden - you gained it for a reason. We ask that you use it now."

"And if I destroy everyone and everything around me?! If I turn out to accidently slaughter all who are near me?! What then?! Who would I be if I lost control?! What would I become if could not wield this new power? It is dark and it dangerous. It so much more than a sorcerers and Niklas himself would be stunned to know what I can do. Perttu might turn his back on me for being so dangerous to his family. I would never see them again if he thought I posed a risk to his children. His mate! I cannot unleash that power. Not for a millennia with Elsa and a child of my own. I cannot."

The table was silent but Joseph had a feeling it wasn't that they were trying to let the information he gave them sink in, it was as though they were pondering on the right choice of words to use to persuade him. It angered him even more so he started to walk away from them. He didn't immediately notice that his eyelashes were wet until something tickled at his chin and he went to swipe at the annoying fly. Only it wasn't a fly. He almost ran there and then, never before had he been so weak and infront of so many. They were ripping open old wounds and he needed air.

"What happened in the white days?"

He heard a gentle feminine voice though he did not recognise it so he knew it was from one of the women who had not yet spoken to him. She spoke so softly to him, he would say hesitantly but he knew that these people were bold in their actions. She was treading tentatively in her tone just to put him at ease.

"Vampires fought vampires." He said.

"What else?"

Dare he say? Should he bring back memories that haunted his days?

"I swam in blood."

"Why 'white' days?"

"Vampires cannot stay in the light but no one could ever decide who would retreat first when the sun came up. So we fought in the sun. We died in the sun. So many burnt under its rays because they would not run away first. Years and it happened every morning. Every morning! I burnt so many times. I do not know why I did not die."

He could feel the heat, the sting, the red hot heat that seared his skin. He could feel it when he spoke of it, remembering the days.

"You fought in the desert?" She asked again.

"Yes. Sand got everywhere. It killed so many because it coated wounds and stuck onto skin. It infected open wounds and grazed already hurt and sensitive flesh. It blunted the hairs on our bodies so we were not the great weapons we used to be. We cannot sharpen our body hair to knives again and wounded and dying I had no choice but to coat my body in wax and pull the hair from my body so it might grow again, sharper. Many of us did that... none survived to do it as many times as I did."

His back was still facing the graceful people. He didn't know if he could turn back to them. He knew his eyes would look dead. He felt dead.

"But Joseph, the blades on your body now are better are they not? Have not they changed as well?" The unknown woman asked.

"They never blunt. I fought in sand years and years later. The sand did not affect them as it did in the white days. They do not shed, they do not fall out anymore. They are so sharp sometimes even I cut myself on them when they are laid down."

And that brought with him another fear. What of the safety of Elsa? Would he ever be able to hold her?

"Can you face the sun?"

"A little but the sun brings back memories I cannot bear. It blinds my eyes and I cannot see anything but the memories of those days. I let Perttu go and rescue his mate in the sun alone because I was too weak. I told him it was the sun that would kill me when really it was my mind. It wouldn't let me torture it so. I betrayed my cousin, my brother, in that moment when my weakness meant I had forsaken him."

It was yet another shame that would never leave him.

"Do you not want all this to end? Do you not want peace Joseph? A different life than this?" The enchantress cooed to him.

"I want to be like Perttu but I can't be. I can't be a family man or sleep at night. I cannot dance as Elsa likes to do and I cannot wear a suit like society, and now you, require of me. I can do nothing but what I do all the time. I fight. I was trained to fight and I will die in battle. That is my fate."

"It doesn't have to be like that Joseph." The man who had sat on his right said to him. At this Joseph did turn round. He span round so fast had he been human he would have felt dizzy.

"And what do you know of it?! How do you know?! I can never escape the past. I can never go back and avoid the wars. I do not want to fight but I have no other purpose in life. If I do not fight physically then my mind does anyway! I am always back there. Every day, every night I am plagued with images of those days. Yes is does have to be like that because I cannot change my own damaged mind! I can't be who you want me to be, this diplomat who is great and skilled and will surely show them all the error of their way. I am a broken soldier and I shall continue in that duty until the end."

"Then you give up on everything else." "It is simpler that way."

He turned and walk away. Not knowing the forest he didn't know where he was going. All he knew was that he couldn't stay with these people a moment longer. He needed air to breathe with and hell, he wanted the heavens to open and let rain pour down on him and drench him. The rain would hide his tears.

Elsa was yet again trying to converse with another man who ignored his tea and looked so pompous she was getting annoyed just looking at him. Her breasts were covered but her dresses had daring necklines and she felt rather uncomfortable as once again man after man sat down besides her and spoke to her like she was a stupid child while looking greedily at her chest. She wanted to grab their faces and pull their heads up so they looked at her face but she knew the etiquette required and her father was observing her. It angered her that he saw the many men look at her chest and he did nothing to stop them. He was totally unconcerned that his daughter had become a show.

She had no desire to marry a single one of them. Rich boys with no thought to any but themselves and in her they say money. In them her father saw business which also meant money. She took in the silver toped cane that this one gentleman held in his hands. One leg was crossed over the other and he wore a fake smile that showed his teeth. He looked the part for such a fake life. She would not make him a good wife. She would get angry at him too often and avoid him all the time. She would not want to raise her children to be like him and she was sure to anger him by attempting to raise the children her own way. But her father was subtly nodding at her to speak with this man more. She could see the eagerness in her old man's face. This was the man her father wanted her to accept so she politely offered him a little cake, which he declined, and tried to carry on the conversation. It was a dead end.

Once the man left her father scolded her for her cold reserve and she was soon greeting yet another one. This time she was pleasantly surprised. His smile was not fake and he didn't once glance to her neckline.

"Alexander Miss. I am very pleased to meet you."

"I am Elsa, please come through. Would you like some tea?"

"Thank you, yes I would."

He followed her through the house commenting on the décor as he went. He seemed to like it. This was going to be an easy one. She could converse with this man and she was even more surprised when he sipped at the tea and accepted one of the offered cakes. Yes this man was very amiable. She beamed at him.

"So your father wants you married?" He asked her.

"Yes, he thinks it's about time now."

"My mother is the same. She wants grandchildren. I keep telling her she will have to wait a few more years but I like to entertain her."

He was going to be her choice if Joseph did not come back. She liked him already. Pity her father didn't, he had taken to scowling already.

"What do you, if you don't my asking?"

"I am trying to take on my father's business at the present, I hope to take It on once I am married and settled. My father is eager to retire from it but wouldn't hear of me taking over until I am comfortably settled."

"That's nice of him."

"Yes, he always is looking out for his children. He got my sister married as soon as she asked him for suitors. Man didn't even make a fuss if it, he asked her how old she was and then nodded. Two days later she was greeting suitors and having a very good time flirting."

A little forward of his sister Elsa thought but then again she had heard the sister in question was happily married in an amicable agreement with lots of servants, a little one on the way and a holiday home in Devon she was to depart to for the birth and consequent confinement months afterwards. That had been a good match.

It was weird but the more they chatted the more it seemed that they connected. He drank more tea and she even called a servant to bring another pot through to them. And he ate another cake. It was a sign that he was comfortable talking to her and he wasn't putting on any false manners but being totally himself. It was a pleasant difference. Her father eventually grunted and left the room leaving her to be chaperoned by Sasha who stood at the back of the room as inconspicuous as possible.

"Do you want to be married?" She finally asked him.

"I think it time I got my head out of the clouds and settled down. I have tried to avoid it for a long time now but I think it best if I start my family and take over the family business. I'm not getting any younger and neither is my father."

"Such an honest answer, I haven't had much honesty this morning." "That is one thing I won't do; deceive. I can never remember the lies and loopholes I say anyway so it's better if I just stick to the truth, it's less trouble in the long run." He chuckled a little at his own luck and sipped more tea. "Miss Elsa I would ask that you allow me to visit with you once again this week. I have to say I have thoroughly enjoyed tea with you today."

"It would indeed be very nice to speak with you again."

He stood up and picked up his hat turning around in a circle to find the cane he had put down and forgotten where.

"Here it is." Elsa said holding it out to him.

"Much obliged." He murmured making for the door. Elsa was following behind him ready to see him out but he suddenly stopped. She almost walked into him.

"One thing before I go Elsa, I wish to know one thing."

"And what is that?"

"I want to know if I have your attention? I do not want to spend the follow week wooing a woman who has set her sights on another man. Can you guarantee me a chance at your affection? Can you guarantee that there is chance of a match at the end of this or do you see me an object to occupy your father's eyes for a while?"

The world was not a nice place to live in. She had to think of her future. Of the future of her dear sister and brother. She had to be reasonable... sensible. She had to place herself in society once and for all, or lose everything.

"...You have my attention Alexander."

Chapter 8

His shrewd eyes glared at her for a whole minute before he tipped his hat at her and left the room. She hastily called for help back to her chair when she felt her legs go weak and tears start to brim in her eyes. "I'm sorry Joseph." She whispered into the air.

Joseph lifted up his hand bringing with it little rocks. He did not touch the jagged surfaces of the stones, nor feel the gritty earth on his fingers. This was his magic. It was to him so simple to lift his hand and bring with it stones. He knew he had the power to bring trees with it. To rip up the earth... And it frightened him.

Stones were one thing; if he lost control they fell back down, they were so small that at most they would graze a little skin if they connected with someone. If he were holding a tree and lost control he would kill those under it. If he ripped up the earth he could send people falling through the cracks and down into the depths of the very planet itself.

To fight in a suit, for Joseph, would not be completely pointless. Maybe that was what they were getting at; soldiers were naked as a rule and he would stand out and shock his opponents if he wore clothes. He was rarely seen on the battlefield anyway, by any side, he was his own man; scouting and destroying the threats.

He rotated the floating rocks so they switched places and then plucked a flower from the ground with his mind only. He could feel the flow of magic through his veins, that current of power that slid through his blood and flesh. He had seen Niklas do extraordinary things. As a sorcerer Niklas had the magic full pelt and he had caused an earthquake in the terrible battle years previously between vampires and hounds. He had fell trees and tore the earth up but that had been his greatest feat and he had needed to concentrate whole heartedly on his task at hand. For Joseph that would be a training exercise.

He let the flower stand in the air in the middle of the rocks so that it seemed to grow up from between them. This was, but a, whisper of his mind, of his concentration. It took up so little strength that he soon got angry. It was irritating more than anything, a niggle in his brain. He kept his darker side hidden for good reason and now they wanted him to let it out?

The rocks dropped to the floor, the flower fluttering down after them, lighter; falling softer back down to the grass. He had the power to pull the ocean onto land and to drain seas of their water until land was in their place. No one man should have that kind of power and he had not asked for it. It had been forced onto him. No... he had developed it, out of necessity. To keep him alive.

"I have connections."

He whipped round falling from his perch which was a rotting tree trunk.

"Enchantress." He acknowledged.

"I have many connections and ways of getting in touch with people. Let me train you. Let me make you into the weapon you have become."

"I do not want to be a weapon!"

"I know you don't. So I'm going to use that tortured mind of yours to keep you under control. To make sure you do not forget the reason why we are developing your powers even more."

"You could corrupt me so easily."

"You could corrupt yourself. But I will not live through any more war, it wearies me and I am not even a part of it. I wonder what it must do to you."

He shook his head and faced away from her.

"It takes the shine from your eyes Joseph and you have a mate now, you cannot go to her as a broken man."

"I don't have a mate."

At this she laughed at him. "Are you so oblivious to the world Joseph that you see past the obvious? There has been one woman on your mind since you left her. That is not the sign of mere curiosity and you shouted her name as your defence in that conversation. Always you want to go back to her. Elsa is your mate Joseph so step up and be one. Learn to control all your power so there is never any danger to her, and stop these wars quickly; so you can retire and spend the rest of your days with her."

Well that did sound tempting.

"You have no idea what I can do."

"Oh you'd be surprised. Joseph you are offending me now, turn around and face me."

Her scowl did nothing to dampen her beauty. He found himself staring her in the eye as that seemed to be the only normal thing about her glowing persona. Her eyes were green. Green like the moss that covered the tree he had been leant on.

"I know what you fear but do you think I would be so careless as to put others in danger? Especially my kin that have come to see you? Do not think me a child Joseph? I have lived longer than you think, and have seen more than you know. Trust me Joseph; as we are going to trust you with our very lives."

"But-;"

"No, Joseph give me a chance. If it isn't working out you can go back to your moody self and never again see me or mine again. You can walk away knowing you were right all along but give me a chance to change your mind. I ask that you come back here the tomorrow night and all will have been prepared for you."

He had loved once. A long time ago and he had seen her walk away from him with a laugh that told him that he had meant so very little to her. It pained him to know that he could be betrayed by a woman so easily. He had spent a year being ruthless; he had built up the failing business of his father and had gained higher prestige amongst his peers. But that one set mind, that pure and utter determination to think of nothing but cut throat business, had wearied him until he had hired someone else to do that part of his job. Now he did the more boring things. Now he oversaw everything that went on but had very little to do with it. The cowards way really but he found that while she had hurt him very much, his anger at her could not last. And it was that passion that had made his work into the success it was.

He walked around the office floor, the heel of his shoe clicked as he wandered. He was not being betrayed this time, nor played. But he was unfairly taking advantage, he had not meant to. He held papers in his hand, important documents regarding money and yet they felt so... frail and inconsequential between his fingers. He had asked for a commitment and he had received one but the look in her eye told him that he was not the only one she had on her mind.

To know that this time he had a woman, he had the dreams of a being a married man with children and a son to take over his business one day. A little girl whose debut he would fund and who he would have to pay a dowry for but ultimately would teach to horse-back ride and converse in French. He longed for the days of bachelorhood to be long past; it was long overdue in his eyes but he saw that it wasn't what she wanted.

He could provide well for her, he would see she wanted for nothing. But it wouldn't be enough. This was one woman whose heart was not swayed by money and whilst his respect grew with that notion, it also grieved him. He could woo her all he liked but that longing in her eyes, for someone other than him, would always be there. He knew that longing and he knew it would never fade. He would never have a woman of his own.

He threw down the papers in his hands. He no longer cared for them. Tomorrow perhaps he would take them up again; today he was going to walk around the park. His legs needed exercise and his mind needed preoccupying with something other than woman and money...

The army of soldiers were resting and refreshing themselves. The down side was that whilst they were doing that they were also contemplating where to go next in their battles. Some were going to travel over to France were they needed more numbers up in their north. A battalion was being dispatched to travel to Switzerland and yet another was bound for Italy. The majority were staying in

England, but were being joined by another army - a bigger one, which had also given numbers to other countries.

In was as Joseph sat down to listen to their plans did he come to understand the enchantress' words. The fighting was not stopping, nor dying down. It was going on and on and alliances were scattered across countries so the irony of it was; that of all the vampire armies of England, half were being dispatched to fight in the same war, against the same people with the landscape being the only difference.

It was ridiculous. The white days were looming in his mind and he wondered when it would come to a head again. One day the fighting would become so ferocious that they would once more go away from the world of mortals to fight amongst themselves in a devastating bloodbath. Another Joseph could not be created, he had restraint and while he didn't want the power given to him another might; and the power he had was too devastating to give to a careless soldier.

In his mind the scene unfolded, all the vampires marching to the deadly, deadly sound of slicing knives through the air. Mortals had drums, vampires used their hair; they whipped it about, throwing their heads around to make the blade-like strands cut through the air and make that terrible whistling sound. He did not want to walk into the battle to that sound again. A sick feeling overtook his stomach and the thought of feeding now was long from his mind. He needed to feed though.

The sound was in his head, he could hear it, hear the slicing, see the heads lolling and the wild appearance of crazed vampires. There was no control, no order, just naked bodies ready to slaughter any who wasn't on their side. And in the midst of battle no one looked too closely at faces anymore, killing one's own comrade was common; barbaric but inevitable in that situation where anything near you was armed with blade and claw and power enough to hurt without touching at all. It was a mess, nothing more. And it never ended, it never stopped until the cries of death by sun were blindingly loud and all were forced to flee at once, together, for a few hours only. The only time they worked together was when the sun was at its highest and even then one would kill their best friend if it meant getting out of the sun.

"Joseph! Joseph?"

He snapped his head around, one of the men, a high ranking one was stood to his side looking confused. "Did you hear a word of that?"

"No, sorry."

"I asked if you were staying in England or making your way somewhere else? We could do with you on our side if you are not due anywhere else."

"I'm staying."

"Ah then you fight with us?"

"... I am undecided where I am needed most as of yet. I will inform you when I know more."

He stood abruptly and made his way away from them all. Aware of all the staring the quiet muttering he just wanted to stay away from those he had called his comrades. He started to run. He felt trapped. He didn't want to stay with his own kind and he was scared to go into the forests in case he was forced once more to do what he didn't want to.

All this over space. Over feeding grounds and money. He shook his head. Perttu was a leader, in charge of many people, a whole area of vampires. The country was split into many areas and each had a leader. Joseph stood for democracy, he stood for the leaders ruling but as whole joining together to discuss common matters. Let vampires be alone, let them live their lives as they wished joined only by common lore. His rivals however, wanted hierarchy. They wanted a prince, a leader of all. They wanted social status and prestige. They wanted a world under one dictator and he knew that dictator. Their potential prince wanted to wipe humans from the face of the earth creating instead half breeds, good only for feeding from and little else. Social order and an end to warring was the 'prince's' policy. Oppression to almost all but a select elite was the reality.

Joseph thought back to Perttu now, he had stayed away from fighting as much as was possible since the birth of his children but he wasn't against fighting if it was necessary. Perttu was a great leader, an impressive soldier himself and Joseph took it as an honour to fight besides him. He wondered if he should call Perttu down to join him in this. But no, the children must come first. And Lily. Lily would not sit idly by and let her husband fight, not after she had found out the grace and fatality of the woman folk. It was too dangerous. Far too dangerous to bring Perttu and woman into this.

The forest by his side looked welcoming. It looked safe and it looked peaceful. Would a day's sleep in such tranquil surroundings be that bad? Would it condemn his fate and make it so he had no choice but to do what the entrances wanted when he woke?

"You can stand there all day debating you fears Joseph of you can come inside and let me show you where you may sleep soundly tonight. The pressure will be on you whether you join us or not, it will not increase or decrease should you stay here. Join us."

By the edge she held out a hand. It looked ethereal, a pale, shinning hand jutting out from the tall lush trees. It looked like a wonder itself and he found himself walking towards it.

"Come Joseph. Have peace , for tonight at least."

He woke, the day had gone and the moon had risen. He knew that the vampires had moved on now to go to their various battles. He stood up from his resting spot and looked around. Clean clothes were hung over the bough of a tree and he made his way slowly over to them. Let him now see these 'provisions' they had brought in order that he might become a trained man. He bathed for as long as he could in the stream before he knew he was taking too long. Their impatience was not going to start the conversation off in a friendly tone.

He donned the tunic shirt and the trousers and looked about, as soon as he had lifted his head, to wonder at the way in which he was supposed to go, he saw a bluebell flower lean ever to slightly to its left. Left it was then. He saw no path as he went in that direction; in fact he saw no animal or creatures at all. He heard no insect chirping or the crunch of leaves. All was silent and undisturbed as he walked by. The most unnerving of all though was that every now and then a flower would lean a certain way. Very subtly it seemed but the flower themselves were directing him - with no sound at all.

Still he said nothing. He needed to feed soon and he wondered if they might have someone willing to lend him their neck for a few minutes. He never took too much, he preferred to feel a little run down as it made using his powers feel bothersome. The fuller he was, the more inclined to test them he became.

It was the faint shimmering of gold that told him where they all were and sure enough the tall yet thin men came to greet and lead him (equally as quiet) to the enchantress who was wearing a beaming smile.

"You look like a Cheshire cat." He greeted to her, forgetting his manners. He expected hell to break lose and he stood tense whilst contemplating who would attack him first for his insult. But the strange thing was that the enchantress laughed. It was a little high pitched and soon over but it set him at ease and brought smiles to all the other shinning men and women around him.

"Joseph, I trust you are rested?"

"I am."

"Are you willing to train? To do as we ask?"

"I still don't know yet."

She smiled again, and turned to her right where, with her hand held out, she showed him something. Something he couldn't quite see. He strained his eyes and looked back at her puzzled when all off a sudden he heard it. Footsteps. Familiar footsteps.

"As one of the people who restored to me my legs, I would gladly lay them down again to aid you Joseph."

His eyes widened, he had not expected him, not in a million years, this was Perttu's friend, Joseph had had little dealings with him save that one act. But sure enough he looked up at the sorcerer Niklas and saw that Niklas himself held a glint in his eye that warned that he too had a few tricks up his sleeve.

"I have other friends you know Joseph." Stepping to the side Niklas revealed a whole horde of people, some were shot and round like dwarves though he had never seen one before. Others were old and hooded and some were hiding behind trees. "I bring you the best magic wielders I could find, though some are a little shy. They stay out of the wars Joseph for the same reason you do not use your powers. They have the power to do terrible things. To become terrible people. But here in the safety of the Enchantress's presence we will come together to share with you all our techniques. Meet Joseph your 'holders'"

Holders. They had the power to bind him? He could be stopped? Even if he got too powerful? He looked Niklas in the eye.

"Is there hope?"

"There is much hope my friend."

Chapter 9

The clouds had covered the moon and it was pitch black amongst the forest, so it was a very good beginning to the lesson.

"Move the clouds Joseph." Niklas said. It was with an audience that he finally let loose on everything that he held so tightly within.

"Don't think badly of me."

"Joseph, I'm jealous! But I know the burden. I do not think badly of you. Now move the clouds so we might have light."

He sighed. Looking up at the heavens he knew that sorcerers used wind to blow the clouds away. He didn't need to do that; he could command the wispy white shapes without needing anything to aid him. He drew in a breath and lifted his hand. Magic flowed inside of him, inside every particle of his body. All he had to do was push it out. Slow and precise were the skills needed at this bit and it required much more concentration. Magic had a tendency to leave his body all at one; the hard part was that utter control needed for delicate procedures. He pushed slowly at the current in his body.

That was what magic felt like, a little current in his bloodstream that he could always feel and was always aware of.

The clouds in the night time sky slowly drifted to the side and moved out of the way of the moons rays.

"Good, that was rather well controlled but how about something heavier."

"The heavier it is the harder I am at controlling it."

"I know that. So lift that tree."

Joseph looked at the old and gnarled tree with knots at the bottom of its trunk leading to the floor. He could lift it far too easily but he had to do it slowly or he could pull out the entire ground the roots covered. He could create a hole in the middle of the very forest.

"Don't worry." He heard a reedy voice behind him, it was thin and old and Joseph turned to it and smiled an old man who was staying far back but watching closely. "We are here if you need to be reigned in."

"Thank you."

He nodded and looked to the tree, lifting his hand he made a gesture from bottom upwards with his palm flat and facing the sky. The tree lifted instantly. Its roots travelled far under the ground, deep down and far away; always searching for more water. He knew what he needed to do; he had to keep the forest intact. So with his other hand he held it out palm facing the floor. Very slowly he pulled his finger inwards so they almost closed his hand. Then he stretched them out again and repeated the action while moving his hand in the general area of a bundle of roots.

In time he had pulled the roots together, huddled them in a ball at the base of the tree and then eventually pulled the tree up, roots and all, forest intact.

"Good! Good! Now put the tree back." Niklas commanded. So this time instead of drawing his fingers inwards he pushed them out, put the tree back in the ground and spread out his fingers unwinding the roots and sending them back to their places beneath the earth and near their water source. He was rather proud of the control he had used and turned back to Niklas looking rather pleased with himself. "There see, that wasn't so hard was it. You have good control for the small things. Shall we move on? Let's see if you can move the ground and control the sea shall we."

"What?"

"The beach is this way. Clouds and trees are beginners level."

He laughed at his relief, looks like he wasn't past the worry then. He followed the sorcerers out of the forest and over to the sea where he had to learn how to control tide, how to lift water, stop waves from crashing down and how to push back the waves from the shore. He had to learn to make the water creep like snails up onto the sand and keep the grains from moving an inch. He was to locate a crab from the deep sea and bring the crab to the land and put it back where he found, all without stepping a foot into the water. Niklas said when he mastered all that he had to move the cliff an inch into the water and back again. The point was not him doing the actions; those he could do very well, it took very little strength to do such things. The point of the exercises were control. It wasn't about moving the water, that was basic, it was moving the water slowly. It was making the waves fall back to the sea bed with the lightness of a feather falling to the floor. The immense power he had meant that he could make waves crash and cause a tsunami if he lacked the apt control. Everything was about moderation. And since he had so much more strength than them, a lack of control would lead to even more disastrous consequences than they could imagine.

Looking around at how many sorcerers had been brought along and the fact that the enchantress and her kin were still around and watching him carefully, told him that it would require all of their combined power to stop him should his control waver but an inch.

He was coming back today and she was dressed in her finest dress. Her hair was tied up high and curly and a little lock was displaced purposely to hang by her neck. It was a taunt. She looked in the mirror and wished that Joseph could see her appearance now. She wished he could be the one she was greeting for afternoon tea but it wasn't. It was Alexander. She was dressed to her very very best because she knew that he was the one she would choose of all the suitors and she had to chose soon. She hoped that Alexander would issue the proposal that would get things moving. Her father had tried to make her sit a full hour with a man twice her age and who constantly looked at her breasts. She hated to be under his gaze. Alexander, while not eh love of her life, would be her salvation in this harsh world where marriage for love was rarely an option.

He was punctual. But then he too wanted a woman just as desperate as the situation with her father was. The top of his cane was polished to a shine and he used it to aid his walking. Though he did not need it he used it, it added to his dignified look. The minute he got inside however he cast it aside and sat down rather ungracefully. She liked that about him, it meant that when they were married there would be no airs and graces within the household. She did not want to be forever on ceremony to her own husband.

"And how are you, my dear, today?" He asked promptly.

"I am well thank you. And yourself?"

"Ah, I have had enough of my work for a while. I am thinking of a holiday soon. A long holiday. Tell me, have you visited the ribbon shop anytime recently?"

"No I have not. I've been keeping to the house since the weather is turning colder. My father thinks it more proper that I do so anyway."

"Ah, well get yourself to the shop my dear. I am having a ball at my house next week; you of course are invited as my very own guest. You family will of course join us?"

"They would indeed."

She waited for the question. Held her breath for it. This would be a marriage of convenience for both of them. 'Say it.' She thought, 'say it and get it over with.' Joseph was not coming back, do not let her heart hurt for much longer. She needed to get over him. She had to please her father, secure a good marriage for the family name and make sure if the worst of the worst happened she could provide for her sister should she not get a husband in the next few years. She had to be practical and now she silently begged that Alexander do her the courtesy of making it quick and simple and easy.

"Elsa?" He began. "The ball I hold, I hope, will be a celebratory one. I have spoken to your father already this morning. Now we are in private I hoped to ask a question of you."

"What is it Alexander?"

She knew what he was asking but she had to play the part, as he was playing his. It was all etiquette. He stood up gracefully and very slowly got down on one knee, his back still straight. He held out a hand and she placed hers in it. He was asking.

"Will you do me the honour of becoming my wife?"

"I will."

It was done. She was engaged. The ball was set. Her mother insisted on a trip to the ribbon shop immediately and to the dress makers. A new dress for the celebration of their engagement was required and the neighbourhood had found out by mid-afternoon. The gossip was flying and everyone wished her well the day after when she went into town. She should have been happy. She should have breathed a sigh of relief to know that she was secure in life now, and that she would be beside a good friend. For Alexander had similar tastes to her. He was amiable and likable. She liked him as a good friend. This marriage would be alright. She had nothing to fear by it but the image of Joseph was in her mind. His letter was still sitting on her bedside table and she found that she looked at it every single day as she got out of bed and got back in.

She would have to burn the letter before the marriage. If anyone found it then her reputation would be gone. She would be ruined. But it was too hard. She could barely touch the paper knowing what she had done. Knowing how she had betrayed his trust. He thought she would wait. But she couldn't. Not this long. Not anymore.

She cried herself to sleep for two nights and started preparations for the wedding the day after. She thought of the flowers she wanted, the dress she was likely to wear and of course her bridesmaids who would stand beside her. For once she was her father's favourite child. He was making a good business partner and she would be out of his hair before long. Apparently, everything was good.

Chapter 10

By the time he had lifted a crab out of the water he had realised that he was still not subtle enough. The crab was crushed, the magic he had used to cocoon it and bring it towards him in a net of sorts was too tight around the crab, too heavy and it had killed the sea creature. He put it back in the place he got it from and tried again feeling around the sea bed for another crab. He had lifted the whole of the sea water that he could see from shore to as far out as the eye can see but he had needed Niklas and six others to contain it. He did not put the water down carefully enough and it crashed back into the sea all at once creating waves too big for him to know how to control.

They yelled orders at him, telling him to push the waves back down, he tried his best but he was doing no good with his heavy handed magic and in the end he had kicked a stone into the water and yelled that this was a bad idea.

"I can hardly feel my magic! Lifting water is so trivial I cannot feel how heavy it is! I don't know what is too harsh or too light. I can't judge it!" He yelled.

"Why do you think we are here? Why do you think I am making you do childish training? Because I know, Joseph, that to you, you need lessons in being graceful and refined and restrained. As a child I had to learn how to be stronger, you need to learn how to be weaker with your power. You are not going to get it in one night, especially since you have refused training all these years. Practice. Do it again."

Niklas had no time for Joseph's moaning or outbursts of temper. A little further up north than they were he had heard tell of a great battle and had decided that it would be the first battle that joseph would go to. They had to prepare him quickly.

"Joseph!" One of the sorcerers called to him when he brought back another dead crab. He looked up, clearly frustrated but trying. "Can do you do press ups?"

"What?" He asked puzzled, "of course I can."

"Good, get down and do five."

He was about to question the order when another sorcerer tutted at his side. Quickly changing his mind about the questioning he laid down on the floor, curled his toes and put his palm on the floor. He pushed up through his hands to his biceps and while remaining horizontal came up, went back down, came up and repeated until he reached five. "Good." The same sorcerer said again. "Now take you hands and feet off the floor. Float."

He had an idea where this was going and wasn't looking forward to it. Using his power he floated in the air about eight inches off the ground. "Good, now do press ups, hands and feet free."

"Will you fix my nose when I smash into the floor?"

"After you give me fifty."

It was nice to know the old men could have a right laugh at him while he slowly let himself float downwards to an inch from the ground and up again to the original eight inches. The push up was fine, it the relax down that wasn't The first time he managed it, and it took a lot of effort. The second time he didn't manage to stop himself as his power got too much a hold over him and he smashed into the floor. Laughter erupted around him but he was determined.

"First rule or learning control." The old man said. "Hurt yourself before other creatures. I couldn't bear to see another dead crab. Besides, my father made me do five hundred magic press ups every morning before school. And I had to fix my own nose."

Two weeks went by. Joseph joined no wars. He declined all mental calls requesting for his backup saying he was needed elsewhere and wouldn't be able to make the battle. Slowly he was becoming an annoyance to his kind. Now he wasn't doing as they wanted and aiding them as they called, they were getting angry at him and started to ask him with a less than friendly and polite tone. That was too much. He was older than many of them. More skilled than all of them put together, or they would not be asking for his help. A little courtesy and respect was needed but he kept his calm, because now he was getting the hang of his magic he was seeing the light at the end of the tunnel. He was seeing the reason he was doing all this for. Let them get angry at him, it would matte little in the end.

His press ups were getting easier. He had yet to cause a tsunami and Niklas had even praised him in earnest the other day when he brought a live crab from out of the sea. He started to run using magic to control his limbs. Too much magic and he would strain his ligaments and tendons inside and it hurt. He started to sleep floating because it exercised the unconscious part of his mind, strengthening his awareness of the current running through him.

If he fell in the midst of his dreams he woke up from the sudden impact on the ground and he would begin all over again.

The first few days had been spent working out the anger he had built up over years and years or war and hiding. The sorcerers told him he needed to make peace with the white days because they were holding him back but he couldn't. It was too terrible to think about them even by mistake. He was not going to purposefully think about them. He had almost crumbled the entire cliff when they dared to bring up the horrendous days when he was wielding magic. They had huddled around him and shielded everyone from falling and crashing rocks - but only just. Then he created the rule: no talking of the white days, especially when he was training. It was simply too dangerous. For all intents and purposes they obeyed that rule but he had a sneaking suspicion that it wouldn't be for long.

He was improving but only just. It would require a few more weeks of intense training before he was acceptable. And he was feeding. It scared him but the sorcerers took it in turns every night to feed him up and build his strength. The more his strength increased the harder it was to control his magic because his magic was growing in strength as well. Since those days fighting in the desert he had never since been at his complete strongest. And so now, when he was getting there, he wasn't used to even his own strong and steady limbs.

"How can you have complete control over your power when you are not at full strength?"

"Full strength brings more danger."

"Only when you are not practiced at wielding it. Don't worry we are here."

"And you all almost died the other day with the rocks. I cannot feed."

But the enchantress put him under spells every night and he had to. He fought the spells long enough that she got angry but one night he made of the mistake of fighting the spell when he was about to bite down on a sorcerer's neck. What should have been a painless bite hurt the man greatly and the spell bound him so he fed hungrily until full. Only afterwards could he apologise. The sorcerer had no complaints but warned him that he would only hurt others if he did not let the enchantress have her spell, and if he did not fulfil the training to his upmost best. After that he did as he was told. It meant that he had a greater chance of keeping people safe.

"Right then, I am off." Niklas announced one day.

"What? No. You can't."

Niklas was his guide. He offered consoling words when training was getting to him. Niklas was his friend not just a mentor like the other sorcerers were. He knew of Niklas's power while he had not seen any of the others' real strength. He trusted this whole confounded plan because of Niklas's presence and now, to see him go made Joseph panic.

"You will be fine, trust my friends here. They will rein you in. I will be back in a few days."

"Where is it you are going to?"

"Don't ask so many questions Joseph. I am going where I am needed and will be back when I am needed as well. Practice!"

With that Niklas walked off. Just walked off with a quick wave of his hand and Joseph was left standing in a circle of people that were staring at him.

"Why has he gone?" He asked the enchantress.

"Because there is something important he must do."

"What is that? I am too dangerous to be left by him."

"He has not left you for long. Calm yourself the water is bubbling."

It actually was, his fear was causing his power to let loose with no control.

"I'm a danger. I didn't know I was doing anything. He needs to come back." For the first time in years Joseph lost it. He did not fear battle, death or anything else but this abandonment in the middle of everything he was doing was too much. He felt himself go to pieces inside and a tree suddenly fell.

"Joseph!"

The old man who taught him to do press up, Jaol, was his name looked furious. He had a hand raised in the air and it was evident he had saved them all from the fallen tree. "Stand up! You are losing control, you can feel yourself becoming dangerous and you sit there doing nothing! Go for a swim, exercise, yell. Do something to stop yourself losing it. As for you fear and panic what do you think we are here for."

"I'm sorry... I just..."

He couldn't explain it.

"Go and sit in the sea. Count your breaths and move the waves to your breathing. Inhale and bring the waves to your chest. Exhale and send them out again. Go now, you have twenty minutes reprieve." His break was still work but as he submerged himself in the water he felt a calmness overtake him. The water lapped gently at his skin and he was able to think logically again. He concentrated on his breathing and brought it back down to normal and then he made the waves come to him and away from him until it because a game. He enjoyed the tiny splash as they hit his chest and if he went too far they hit him in the face. So he started to have fun. One on the chest, one on the face, one on the chest, one on the cliff.

Back on the shore everyone watched as he slowly calmed down and then started to test himself better. To play.

"He never had a childhood did he?" One of the enchantress' kin asked. A man with blonde and very tall.

"No." The enchantress said. "When his father died he lost his ignorance of the world and shunned the chance of a happy childhood, with his cousin Perttu, for the harsh independent world of adults. He started training then. Playing is something lost to him. He needs to remember that innocence before this is over, or he won't be able to save anyone... Not even himself."

Chapter 11

Her mother had taken control of her wedding. What she wanted had changed to what was appropriate and what the 'guests' would want to see. The guest list itself was out of her hands but after seeing the length of paper her mother was using to write the list she knew it was going to be a large reception.

She had wanted a plain dress, new and edged nicely with lace but essentially plain. Her mother was insisting on detail. Lots of detail and embellishment. In short, Elsa was beginning to think her mother was trying to make a show out of her and it didn't please her one bit. She tried to apologise to Alexander for her mother's going over the top but he only laughed.

"Mothers will be mothers, let them have their fun. They like to get excited since their own wedding days are long gone." He said he didn't mind one bit what went on throughout the day only, that the vows be said and they exchange rings.

They had tea together every day at four thirty and there they tried to get to know one another a little better before the wedding was to take place. They spoke of the books they liked and the piano pieces they preferred. They spoke of dancing and even ventured into certain philosophical discussions. It was nice to have a man that would allow her the freedom of speaking her mind and didn't mind that she had read books on politics and other religions. She got on rather well with Alexander and as the wedding date was nearing she was pleased. Heart broken, but accepting of her position. She had known girls to have much worse marriage partners and their lives would never be happy. She was glad that at last she would like her husband.

Her new house was grand. She had been taken to visit there and she had to admit, being the lady of such a house was a little daunting but she assumed that once she was married and settled down, that it would seem much better and easier. She wrote to her friends and told them what her new address would be, saying that they must write regularly still and visit as often as they were able.

She had taken to kissing Joseph's letter at night because she knew that the day was approaching when she must burn the evidence of her love for someone else. She felt as if she would like to fold the paper up and place it in a necklace thereby never taking it off and hiding her secret forever away from the world. But it would never work. And she would not start off her marriage to Alexander with such a deceit. She had promised him her attention and he was getting it; one hundred percent when she was in his company. Her heart did ache something terrible though.

Another day dawned and she struggled to get out of bed, too tired to be bothered with the morning routine. But she heard the servants milling about and knew one would come in eventually to try and light her fire or something stupid like that, so she hid the letter under her mirror and climbed stiffly out of bed. Her day did not get better. By teatime she was sat in the parlour with the teapot and staring outside. She was so lost in thought that she did not hear the door knock or even the footsteps which announced that Alexander had come in.

"My my Elsa, you are distracted today."

"Oh! Sorry I was day dreaming."

"I can see that."

He took his usual seat opposite her and let the servant faff around with pouring tea and offering him little cakes, until Elsa told the servant they could manage and she herself took over pouring him his tea.

"Sorry, my mother likes it when they bustle around her; I don't."

"I've become accustomed to your independence since I started to come for tea here. I do not mind it."

He talked evasively of his business, just a little to engage her into conversation but not enough to bore her with details or expect her to understand a world from with she was shunned. She in turn chatted away, as was polite, but today she was more depressed than usual. Her mother had named the date officially and sent out the invitations. She was not aware of herself slipping away again into that distant world that belonged only in her mind, but the feel of something pressing against her lips brought her swiftly back out of it.

"Alexander!" She cried pulling away from his lips. It wasn't right. It didn't feel good to kiss him. It left her feeling oddly cold inside and he was... not as gentle, not as sweet, nor as commanding as the previous lips that had last touched her mouth. "I mean... we shouldn't. We are not married."

She knew it was foolish to pull the marriage card. They were engaged and being caught kissing her betrothed would be only light gossip, nothing too scandalous, especially since the wedding date was set. There was no harm in a little kiss but she used the excuse anyway. Let him think her an innocent and inexperienced maiden. But there was a look in his eye that she couldn't decipher but was afraid to look at too closely.

"I get the feeling that you do not wanting the same as me Elsa."

He picked up his cane and was pulled on his coat. Had she offended him? No she didn't mean to! "I'm so sorry! I am just distracted. The wedding plans have been on my mind for a while and I am over tired with them. Forgive me. I... I am not used to such bold moves. Pray, ignore that. I swore to you that you had my attention."

His hand went to her shoulders and he nodded his head at her. He would leave her to her many thoughts. Bending down he leant close to her ear, she thought he was going to kiss her cheek as men had done in the past to her when she was younger but he didn't. Instead he whispered his departing words to her and left.

"But not your affection."

She had sat, pale and worried in her chair for another hour before she called the servant to remove the tea tray and tell her mother she was going for a walk around the garden. How much did Alexander know? His words had puzzled her. She walked slowly up the stairs, intending to get another shawl, when there was a knock on the door. "Alice." She called to the servant, "if it is Alexander come back, if he has forgotten anything please show him to the room but tell him I have gone for a lie down. I do not feel too well."

"Alright Miss."

She carried on to her room but stopped when she heard a little huffing and puffing behind her. Turning she saw Alice bobbing behind her trying to catch up. "Miss, it's for you. A gentleman by the name of Mr Smith. He says he needs to speak to you urgently about important business."

"Mr Smith? I do not know a Mr Smith. Are you sure it isn't a call for my father?"

"I wouldn't mistake the daughter for the father Miss. Please he seemed rather impatient when I told you had gone for a lie down and I had to fetch you."

"I am coming."

She turned back around and descended the stairs again coming face to face with a man she had never seen before, he wasn't even one of her father's friends or business associates - and she had seen many of them in his study. This man was a little aged and his face was rather stern at the moment. He was and because of that she was wary of getting too close to him; his presence seemed imposing. He was watching her walk all the way down the stairs and he seemed to be timing her steps.

"Good afternoon. I believe you are newly betrothed to a business partner of your fathers?"

"Yes I am."

"Allow me to talk to you for a moment. I won't take up much of your time - if you are an insincere person."

"Excuse me?!"

Was he trying to offend her? She didn't like his choice of words.

"Tea would be nice. Thank you." He said walking towards her own parlour! She hurried after him determined that he wouldn't get tea or even a chair if he was to be so rude. She told the servant to fetch her brother who was in the study and to keep this quiet from her mother, who would shriek shrilly if she knew someone was marching around her house.

Following this impetuous man she called after him, "Excuse me Sir, I have not invited you in. I do not even know your name. You are being rather rude Sir, and I must ask that you leave at once or my brother will be called."

"If you get your brother involved he will only get hurt. As for my being rude, you are the one who has offended me. You Elsa have a mate and Joseph works hard to return to you! And now when I come to bring you to him myself, I find you about to marry another. How dare you?! And as for my name it is Niklas!"

"...Sir, please sit down. I'll ask for tea."

"She ran out into the hallway and called off her brother saying it was a friend of Alexander's and she needed tea and cakes again. It was brought into the parlour straight away and she busied herself in pouring tea for a minute, all the while keeping her face averted from the furious man infront of her.

"Are you going to tell me why it is I come for a single woman and find a taken one?"

"I couldn't help it. My father is trying to marry me off. I had to choose a man; Joseph went away with no explanation and left no date as to when he would come back. Nor an address for me to write a letter to him. No one had seen him but me I couldn't very well tell my father I had a suitor from out of town and who I didn't know a thing about. My father would have disapproved of Joseph anyway... being with him was always going to be hard. I waited as long as I could but my father was putting pressure on me. I gave my word to

Alexander; it was him or... a man who wanted my body and money only. My father's choices were not the best."

The man infront of he was silent for a minute. "You gave your word?"

"I did."

"And would you take it back?"

"I would love to be betrothed to Joseph but he has not asked me and I have the chance of security with Alexander."

She stood up from her chair and walked away. "I will marry a friend. I can have a home and a comfortable life. I'll never forget Joseph. I still have his letter... but I will have to get rid of that soon."

"And what if I said I could take you to Joseph. What if I could promise you that he would give you a comfortable life and provide for you? What if I told you he thinks of you every day and intends to come back for you as soon as his business is done?"

"I am promised to Alexander now. I... promised him my attention."

But not her affection, as he had pointed himself that very day. Could she call off an engagement that had gone all around the neighbourhood? It would be a cruel thing to do for his reputation, a very cruel thing to do. Could she do that to his name? He would be laughed at and whispered about by everyone if the one he asked to marry him broke off the engagements when the wedding dress was already ordered.

"I can't do that to him. Not now."

"Then I must go back empty handed? I must tell Joseph that you sacrifice his happiness and the only hope he clings to in his coming battles, all because the one he loves is thinking about the reputation of another man?"

"Be reasonable. I did not want this! He will get over me in time. I will try to do the same." Though it felt as if that would never happen.

"He will not get over you, he is not human. He does not love like humans love - he has a mate. And that mate is you. You are a vampire's Bride and that means neither of you will stop loving the other. You betray him by going with another man. He will know when you... consummate your marriage. You'll break his heart!"

She looked up at the man infront of her utterly shocked by the venom in his voice and the words that came out of his mouth. Vampire? Mate? What was all this? She looked at the teapot in her hands; she had also had a drink from it before she launched into an explanation. There was nothing in the tea to addle his brain. She didn't understand where his words of madness came from but she now thought it best if he left her to her business. He may know Joseph but he clearly wasn't a stable minded person.

"I'm sorry I must ask you again to leave."

He jumped to his feet and took hold of her arms, shaking her a little. She would have squeaked maybe even screamed in fear but her voice wouldn't work. She opened her mouth but there was no sound coming out. She wriggled in his grip but he didn't let up on her. "Don't believe me? Think me mad? You and he are connected little one and you cannot marry this man! You cannot."

He let go of her then and walked out of the parlour. Even when he had left her sight she heard his footsteps on the floor making his way across the tiles to the front door. It banged shut loudly behind him and her brother began asking what all the racket was. She just said she had a headache and pushed past him to go and lay down. Tears were threatening to fall from her eyes and she threw herself on the bed and took out the letter from under mirror. Why could he not have come for her that day? She would have told him her father was pressuring her to marry. She would have asked him his intentions. She let her tears out and cried silently into her pillow until at last she fell asleep and let everything slip away for a while. Now everything was a mess, a big mess saw no end to.

Chapter 12

Niklas came back in a foul mood. While Joseph had knuckled down even harder in Niklas's absence he was relieved to see him coming back. To think, that during the past few days there had been no sure back up if he failed, he stepped up his own awareness of everything he did. He tried hard to feel the flow of power even when he was using such an inconsequential amount. Lifting himself up from the floor in a press-up cost him hardly any energy and soon he was finding that lowering himself back down also took a lot less hard work. He wasn't sweating as much. He hadn't woken in the middle of the night for two days because he managed to stay floating throughout his sleep, and he had even woke up the next night feeling just as refreshed. His sea creatures were staying alive and getting smaller than the crabs he brought initial. Indeed he floated up a fish the day before Niklas got back and the delicate, slippery thing was still flapping about wildly when it came to the shore. He let it go quickly before it died from lack of oxygen.

He also moved the cliff. He pushed it back and noise of the earth grinding against the ground was loud, deafening in fact and for a second he had thought he had done something wrong. But no, he had simply moved it to the middle of the deserted forest. He had moved a cliff and still wasn't sweating. The sorcerers were impressed and wanted to see if her could do more but there was too much landscape that would be destroyed if he moved it too much.

He had been resting for a while when suddenly Niklas came back and walked past them all without saying a thing, instead he went and stood in the sea. His bare feet stood in the wet stand and made imprints while the rest of him stared at the horizon.

"Niklas?!" Joseph called. "Is everything alright?"

"Everything is fine carry on practising!"

Without looking back at Joseph (Niklas couldn't bare it) he let himself sink to his knees in the water. He lifted up his hands and brought with it a bit of the water. Then, like the pressing of keys on a piano, he moved his fingers up and down to make the waves move in rhythm whilst getting higher and higher until it was at his eye level. Lifting his head, the waves also raised themselves a bit more and from back on the shore Joseph watched, impressed, as Niklas brought the weaves around him and cage himself in revolving water.

"What is he doing?" He asked of Jaol.

"He must be stressed. He is trying to calm down. Let him be. Come on let's see how you are at defending yourself, we know you can attack easily."

Jaol put a hand on Joseph's shoulder and led him away. Back in the water Niklas was glad, he didn't want to see Joseph's face after he found out the most devastating news. He was debating not telling him at all but the wedding night would break him; it might be best to prepare him for the crushing news. He had no sooner thought of that when the waves dropped, he lost his concentration and they sank back down; falling right on top of him and pushing him too far under so his back scraped along the sea bed and he was in danger of being pulled out into the depths of the sea. Just as he was about to anchor himself to the sea bed and regain control of himself he felt a blanket go around him. No; not a blanket, he was in the sea where blankets weren't. He gasped and looked around but all he saw was water. Lots of water and the salt stung his eyes.

The 'blanket' wrapped around him and cushioned him, cocooned him safely and he felt himself lifting in the air. He saw the surface of the water and took in a deep breath to stop the burning of his lungs. He was slowly being floated back to the surface and he was grateful for his friends having saved him. "Thank you." He said coming to the shore but he looked around and then stopped in his hurried speaking. Joseph was stood there holding up his arms.

"Guess I'm improving." Joseph said dryly.

"Thank god, if I had known it was you I would have been preparing myself to join all those crabs."

He stood back up and formerly shook Joseph hand for his aid. "I need to talk to you after you have practised with Jaol." "Alright." Joseph was till frowning when he left his friend. What on earth had caused such a lapse in concentration. Of course Niklas could have saved himself but Joseph wouldn't risk it, not with his good friend.

"I'm going to throw some weapons at you I want you to stop them in the air."

Joseph was stood in the middle of a clearing; his audience consisted of only two others at this point. He was getting better so his holders were getting fewer. Jaol lifted up a sword and two daggers swiftly throwing them at his face. To joseph this was easy, there was no risk of himself getting to hurt; he lifted his hand up and pushed out his power not only stopping them in mid but-;

"Joseph!"

He had pushed them backwards, too far backwards so they hurtled back towards Jaol.

"Sorry!" He called out, anchoring his magic around them and stopping them a hair's breadth away from Jaol's face. His two holders were ready, their hands raised in case he wasn't quick enough but he was. The three blades fell to the floor.

"I said stop them! Not send them back to me. I knew you would do that. Feel that subtle power and do it again, you're too experienced- now I expected you to get it right this time."

He almost did. He only sent them a little way back and Jaol had him practising for a good hour despite him getting the hang of it on his fourth attempt. Jaol wasn't taking any chances. At the end if his practice he saw the sun starting to rise. He still had to talk to Niklas. It was Niklas that was stood by the clearing all ready to talk to him.

"This way."

This couldn't be good. He narrowed his eyebrows and felt his belly start to feel heavy.

"Niklas? What's going on?" He looked around him and was surprised to see that, while he was being given a lot of privacy for this conversation, all around the trees was the faint golden glow. The Enchanters, all the Enchantress' kin were surrounding him at a distance. "Niklas why are they are here?"

"I'm taking you to somewhere it will not matter if you destroy."

"Why?"

"I have bad news Joseph. I need you to keep control of yourself."

They stopped.

"Tell me Niklas."

"I went to see Elsa. I was going to bring her to you but I found out that she is to be married to another. A man called Alexander."

"...No..."

He broke...

...He had always thought that he would go back to her. The Enchantress had told him Elsa was his Bride. She couldn't marry someone else, she was his. She must be feeling for him what he was feeling for her. She had to be. It was impossible not to because of the instinctive bond. All the hope of doing something good, all the plans and all his training, it all seemed to mean nothing. This peace he was fighting for, as slim as it had seemed before now only looked more so. It was as if the world was... one long monotonous night. There was nothing anymore held in it. There were no colours. There was no hope. Or love. Or peace. All there was war, and night time, sixteen hours awake and eight asleep and that was it... There was no point anymore.

His legs went from under him and he was lost in despair, the bond only seemed to hold him in its grip harder, he became overly aware of the feeling of longing for Elsa and the image of her smile and laughter was strong in his mind. Niklas was no longer besides him and it didn't matter. He didn't see Niklas, not even the trees that were slowly falling down and being supported by the magical glowing and graceful creatures in the background. He saw none of this.

The despair left him and, dangerously, anger replaced it until he was raging into the night. Throwing his head back he cried out to the swirling ball of laughing fate. All he had gone through, everything he was, and he was not even allowed the one reprieve given to all other vampires. He was not allowed the female everyone else seemed entitled to. He missed her.

The hair on his body stood to attention and he let the change take over him, let his teeth burst free of his mouth to force his mouth open a little. His great long claws dug deeps lines into the soil and even as he carried on crying out into the night he purposely released the power in himself. They wanted to see what he could do, they wanted to force him to use his powers... then so be it.

He started to pull everything towards him. He stretched his arms out as wide as they would go and in doing so ripped up the trees, all of them, the roots that had grounded themselves so deep under the soil were also pulled up, creating huge holes. He pulled at the stones, the flowers, the rocks and the leaves. Pulling everything from the floor upwards he made them revolve around his head as Niklas had with the sea water. He looked at the clouds in the sky, the sun. He didn't want to see such light so he brought all the clouds over to cover it and hide it. Once that was covered he put the sky back to a darkness that usually reigned at night. He felt the relief on his skin from the sun but its rays still tried to get out. The he did what he said he would never do - he went to pull the water on land.

He felt himself reaching for it somewhere in the distance where he knew it to be. He even felt its weight as it began to obey his command. He pulled... But somewhere at the back of his mind he was aware that it was wrong to be doing this. He roared loudly to the black sky.

"Is this what you wanted?!" He cried to everyone and everything around him. "Is this who you wanted me to be?!"

He tested his power again about to bring the sea to him but he couldn't. Well he could but he knew he shouldn't. Fate may have taken his woman from him but he wouldn't cause more death. He wouldn't take the water from its proper place. If he did drown the entire forest would drown and the water would spread out across the land. People would scream as he was, they would see their loved one die; lose them as he was losing Elsa. But he wasn't losing her to death. Not yet; if she refused to be his Bride then she would not be a vampire and that terrible death day would come soon but for now she lived. He had time to come to terms with the inevitable cycle of life and death for the mortals. Hell he might even join her.

He let go of the sea before he could take it from its bed. He had ripped up the earth and now he careful laid it back over the tree roots that rehomed. He put down the trees, the stones, the boulders and the debris that covered the forest floor. He couldn't however bear to remove the clouds and let daylight blind him again. He didn't want to see the light anymore. They were reminding him of the white days. He had been created a monster with nothing now to hold him back. With no one to take the edge off his nightmares. He was a, purely, wholly, dangerous beast.

He had so much strength left, so much power flowing around his bloodstream still. He hadn't tired in the least and he had just ripped up the entire clearing of its trees. He fell to his knees.

"Allow me to give you relief this day." He heard softly. He didn't look up to know it was the enchantress. He didn't reply to her either, letting her do what she wanted as everyone else, including his mate, seemed to do. Whatever happened he only hoped that he didn't wake up from it.

Chapter 13

Niklas was pacing the floor, it had been three days now since the enchantress had sent Joseph to sleep and now as the sun was shining they had all gathered together to discuss whether it was safe for him to be awoken. They had not interfered when they had seen him pull up ground and pull in sea because he had wavered when he felt the sea under his power. It was as if he was coming back to his senses and so they had given him a chance. Luckily he had come through. But not before he had completely drowned the shore trying to bring the sea inland.

When he had put the water back he may have restored the shore but they had recognised how unstable he was now. It wasn't right that he couldn't be allowed his own mate, especially since it was mere human convention that set the barrier between them. They all wondered at what they would find when he woke up; would it be the depressed Joseph or the angry Joseph that needed to be instantly sent to sleep again.

The irony was that when Joseph woke up he was a changed man. So far changed they were astounded by the sudden transition.

He went about the daily routine as if he was bored. He stopped weapons mid-air and they did not even shiver in the opposite direction. His control had spiked to an all-time high that was the pinnacle of his power. He needed no holders and that was mission accomplished. The effort it took him to use his power was the same lack of effort he needed to also refine and constrain it. But with that change came the devastating realisation that the progress had come a terrible price. Joseph's eyes looked dead.

"Joseph, how are you feeling this morning?"

"Let's just get on with things Niklas."

"No Joseph, tell me. How are you doing?"

"Fine, it's doesn't hurt anymore."

As though in a daze Joseph walked away, the trees on either side shimmered as he walked past the very natural environment shying away from the feel of his power that was brushing at them from his unconscious aura. But he did nothing; the power was there and could be vaguely felt but it did nothing. Not yet. Joseph needed to think. His eyes barely noticed anything. Truthfully it did still hurt him but he pushed it to the back of his mind, so far back that he was beginning to get numb. He couldn't see anything. Elsa had been in his dreams, in his mind and he felt that the more he purposely tried not to 'see' her, in his mind, the more he couldn't really see anything around him. He couldn't appreciate the trees, the sea, or even the grass that his bare feet walked across.

He had stopped wearing his boots when he woke up because he found them cumbersome. He could feel the floor before his feet touched it; he didn't need the protection of such heavy soled shoes anymore. He left his shirt open not wanting the restraint and he let his hair grown that little bit more. He felt freer if his hair was longer and the locks could move in the wind. Niklas was at a loss, he was just glad he had spent the last few days preparing for this. Watching as joseph left them to their selves they all exchanged worried glances. "Not much we can do for him now." Jaol commented feeling a little sad that his friend had now entered the oblivion that came with the loss of a mate.

"Send him to war."

The voice came from the enchantress and even she looked defeated. Her features seemed drawn and her beauty looked strained, as if it was a façade she was struggling to uphold. "Send him to the familiar ground he knows. There is no negotiating when the negotiator can't distinguish between the sides."

"But, he is trained. We have all-;"

"It doesn't matter. Do you think he is capable of a great speech? Do you think he can do anything in this dazed state? Give him three days and he will be like a rabid dog. He will be an assets to the side he fights on. We need a calm man to stop this war, we need someone who can make a difference, he had fallen off the edge of a cliff into an unknown territory and be warned... should the power in him slip out of control, like he soon will, you must all be prepared to destroy him. It has come to an end, we will stay in the forest until it falls, then we will search for another. Our days are not over yet, they are just going to get... very unbearable."

Even as she spoke the words, from out of the corners of the forest came the whole lot of her kin. All the shinning, slender and well-dressed men and women walked out to the trees, their faces were solemn and their own lights were fading. The enchantress' power was so great her light had not faded, but they could tell, the sorcerer's all knew that what they had worked for had just walked away from them.

"You can not give up on him." Jaol insisted.

"He gave up on himself a long time ago, now he believes the world to have forsaken him and so he has forsaken the world. Send him to war, if he fights he will win and he just might remember why we trained him to stop the fighting. Or he might not. We won't know until we send him."

"And until he gets back?"

"Peace Niklas, we wait for him."

"Perttu is on his way."

The forest stilled. "And Perttu's wife and children?"

"Are with him. I went to him because I knew Joseph would need a brother by the end. Perttu insisted on bringing his family; I thought it safe, until I saw his reaction."

"Keep the children from him. Keep the wife from him, he shouldn't see the family he will never have, and the woman and child should not be around someone as dangerous as he is."

"He is in perfect control!" Jaol argued.

"NO! He controls his magic perfectly! But when he loses control of himself he will lost the grip on his magic and he will create devastation." Niklas yelled back.

"... What do we do about them then?" Another asked.

"Go and send him to war now. Perttu can decide what to do when he gets here." The enchantress ordered, eager to avoid a quarrel at that moment. Niklas stepped forward and looked her straight in the eyes.

"Perttu will join his cousin."

"Will he? He is a father now, be warned Niklas, they might not go the way you planned, Perttu's priorities may have changed."

Chapter 14

He was sat on top of a church, crouched solemnly with one hand resting lightly on the slats to steady his posture. The roof of the church was stable enough but he was balanced on one of the many ledges and he knew that should he sway he would fall immediately. The slightest shake of the ground would send him tumbling but still, he stayed on that ledge and watched his kin below. The bloodbath was... beyond words. There were no words to describe the smell of metallic blood splashed everywhere in huge puddles. There was no single word to describe the sick feeling he had in his stomach when he saw flesh scored open by what seemed to be a thousand knives. The staring eyes that looking at the dark clouded sky were empty and lifeless and the expressions on their faces told him all he needed to know.

They were soldiers in a war and hatred gleamed in their expression; hatred for the enemy they fought, unaware that those on the other side may very well have fought on their side at one time. In this very messed up and unorganised war enemies and comrades were not a constant. He saw the panic on their faces when they realised that they had lost, that they had finally succumbed to a death that should never have befallen a soldier of their race. A vampire was meant to live out the ages of the world, to see the changes of season and year and watch as generation after generation of humans died. Vampires were bound to walk the world with their family as their strength, their race as comfort and that one special beloved to take away the memories that haunted them at night.

The roaring of vampiric battle cries was chilling. It was a high pitch feline type of growl and it rolled from their tongues with the ease of water flowing in a stream; only this was not as peaceful. This was the stark difference to the tranquillity found at a stream. In the battle there was one in particular vampire. One who had abandoned his usual techniques, whose skill in stalking and waiting and patiently surveying the scene had been cast aside to let him be the angry animal he was turning out to be.

It was as though Perttu was watching a dream, as he watched his cousin run around the battle field killing efficiently, quickly... far too easily. Killing should never be that easy, or as mindless. The side he was fighting for were impressed, they rejoiced at their blessing of such a soldier but what they did not want to do, was get that close. They did not want to meet this man at the end; they wanted their acclaimed warrior to win the battle for them and then walk away - they feared him. He was not a mere saviour, he was a weapon.

It was his cousin Joseph's horrific war cries that were sent up into the air and any who listened heard only pure and adulterated power and resolve to kill any in his way. But to Perttu... To Perttu who had grown up with his cousin being his brother he heard something far different. He heard the pain behind that cry. He heard the tears that were impossible to shed. He knew that that shriek of terror was a shout to the fates who watched down on them and had taken away his beautiful bride and given a fate unfair to them all.

"Joseph, hear me." He whispered into the night. He made barely any sound but he knew the magic behind it sent it straight to Joseph's ears. He saw the hair on his cousin's back shiver once, like a little evergreen tree would quiver once when a heap of snow fell on it.

Joseph held a vampire in his very hands, its head in his palms and Perttu knew he was being dangerous here, he was distracting his 'brother' who could die by a single miscalculation on that bloody field.

"Come away Joseph." He whispered. "Come away and sleep awhile. You tire from this battle; can you not feel it in your bones?"

With a soothing and calming voice, a balm almost, Perttu hoped to hypnotise his brother from the battle field and take him back to the training in the forests that would put an end to this horror. "Let me guide you to where you might rest. Let me help you. You can lean on me. Look at what you have been through so far, look at the death that clings to your legs. Walk away from it. Come to me."

Joseph stopped, his form held straight, steady and prepared. He was tensed ready for attack and Perttu watched from his high up spot, gripping the stone ledge with so much strength he felt it crumbling under his hold. "Put him down and walk away." He ordered. "Step off this battlefield and join us again. Join us again in this fight for peace."

It was with a semblance of shock that Perttu watched as Joseph turned around abruptly and his eyes landed straight on Perttu's. As if he had known all along he was sitting on that rooftop watching him. He had not succumbed to the power of Perttu's voice.

"Why should I?"

"Have you not killed enough?!"

"Has not every one of us? Have not we all got blood engraved on our hands and the smell forever lodged in our noses? Why should I come away, this war has valid reasons for starting, why not bring about a decision?"

"A decision reached by which side can walk away? Who then go on to fight with the next group with the same agenda, the same disagreements with everyone else?! Do you feel better? Does the pain of losing Elsa go away with every vampire you kill?"

"... It..."

"Does it?!" Long gone was Perttu's civility. "Do you feel at ease at your fated lot now you have killed?!"

"..."

"Answer me!"

"No!"

Perttu felt his heart break. Joseph stood in the middle of the dead, like a demon, and yet so very vulnerable in that moment. "Come to me." He called to Joseph. "Come away from this... Come away from this." With his hypnotic voice Perttu led Joseph from off the battle field and to the front doors of the church where he was taking no chances. He put Joseph into a sleep only family could do to one another to render them less dangerous, and then he lifted up his cousin into his arms and carried back to the forest and towards the sea he had spent so long pulling crabs out of.

"The next bit must be your own choice. Wake and make me proud. Don't let me regret calling you my brother. Come back to us Joseph. I cannot give you your mate but I can make the world that little less harsh."

He put Joseph's sleeping form down on the sand and let his bare feet immerse in the cold water. Then he backed away and left Joseph alone and leaving with Perttu were the sorcerer's, the enchantress and all her kin. They made it so that Joseph was completely, totally, alone...

Chapter 15

He awoke in a rage. A thunderous rage. He had been in battle and that was all he could remember; the blood, the flesh, the pain of biting , scratching and cutting. He could hear the cries of everyone around and he flexed his claws and made to move forward before he realised his claws were retracted, only normal length fingernails were on his hands. He couldn't walk forward because he was lied down and to top it all off - his hair was humanlike all over his body not the knives that battle required and his feet felt cool. If he was in battle his feet were meant to be covered in blood from walking in it and that certainly was not a 'cool' feeling.

He opened his eyes properly to notice the sky was clouded and a few birds were flying overhead. The more he puzzled at the scene his eyes were seeing, the more the noise of battle died down; the sounds of war screams seemed to become more distant until they sounded like that from a memory. Salt air made the smell around him fresh and crisp. It held a cleanliness in the air that on the battlefield would be the opposite – it should be stuffy, overpowering and very very dirty. Which obviously meant that he wasn't on a battlefield. So was he dead? He hoped so, then he wouldn't think about Els-, oh, he couldn't be dead. It wouldn't hurt as much inside if he were dead.

Scrunching up his face he screamed into the night in more anguish. A tickle on his shin made him stop and sit up abruptly. He was by the beach. Still confused he was tempted to try and pull a crab from the water as was his usual routine but there was no one around. He wasn't in training. How had he got off the battlefield and how long had he been here? If he'd lied on the sandy beach through the day then why had not the sun burned him alive? Then it clicked. The only thing that would leave him so confused and made sense was if part of his family had sent him to sleep. But he had no family left... Perttu.

He was furious! He had acknowledged Perttu as a brother years ago, that had no doubt sealed a bound between then, they had become brothers in the eyes of magic and Perttu now had a hold over him. Before he had even thought through the consequences in his own mind he went over to a tree and took hold of it's trunk to rip it from its root with his bare hands as an outlet for his anger. A branch fell from its lofty perch and hit Joseph on the head and the sudden impact of what he was doing slammed into him. He was angry at a man who had saved his life and vice versa so often in the past. Perttu had taken him under his wing, always been there for him and Joseph was repaying that with an act of violence that could quite easily have been Perttu had he been stood where the tree was. What was happening to him? Why was he so angry?

More despair rained down on him and he sank to his knees, replacing the tree back into the ground and letting fall a single tear of blood. It was one thing to be angry at the world but he was hurting people. If Perttu had been there last night then he had witnessed him becoming a machine of slaughter. He had been a beast last night and if Perttu had saved him from more sins he owed his cousin much much more than getting angry at an act of love. Love, he would never have that. He was about to be lost to everything but slowly he heard a voice in his mind. A reiteration from last night and he knew Perttu had taken control of him. Now he heard his brother's voice in his head. The next bit must be your own choice. Wake and make me proud. Don't let me regret calling you my brother. Come back to us Joseph. I cannot give you your mate but I can make the world that little less harsh.

Make him proud. Don't make him regret calling him brother. Looking at his actions Joseph knew it would be a miracle he hadn't already let Perttu down. But how could he make it right? What could he do now?

"How's the kids?"

"Ah they're doing alright. I can't believe how quickly they grow; they need new clothes every few week. Lily loves it because she gets a new dress out of me as well."

"Ah, women, they always know how to twist us round their little fingers."

"Yep, especially Lily, she just has to tell how many hours she was in labour for – the grand total for all four kids – then says I owe her!"

"You did get her pregnant."

"Hey, it does take two you know! My bank balance shouldn't suffer for that!"

The sorcerers that had gathered around Perttu were laughing at his predicament, all eager to know what his little province was like. He commanded a lot of people himself and not one of them had fought in the new wars. They had been scouting instead, trying to gain information about the war but as far as anyone could tell they were a chaotic mess. There was something else though. Something that Perttu couldn't quite put his finger on.

"Perttu? Where is lily?" Niklas asked.

"She is on her way, she is being accompanied by my father, it seemed safer for her. I needed to see how Joseph was before I brought her along."

"And the children?"

"Are coming. Whatever happens I think they have a hold over him that none of us have. He is so different around them. Lily gave birth only a few weeks ago but Joseph changed when Jack was born. He seemed... he didn't hold him but he never stopped looking at him. It was as if he couldn't bear to be close to him and yet I found him guarding the door to the nursery when Jack went down for a nap."

"Perttu, don't you thinks it's too dangerous to bring them, what if he turns? What if he hurts them in one of his rages? What will any of you do if he takes a child from you in his madness?"

"He will kill me."

Joseph emerged from the trees looking Perttu directly in the eye. "If I become capable of such a horror that I hurt an innocent child, then I am not fit to stay alive. I will do right you my brother, and by the family you bring."

"Joseph!" Overcome with joy Perttu ran at him but Joseph stopped him.

"I am dangerous. I need a few days of training to discipline myself. Don't let the kids see me until the week's end. I am so sorry for what I did last night. I'm sorry for everything, I have a task to do and I won't neglect it. Too much depends on the outcome of these wars.

Hearing your voice when I woke, I knew I had to choose my side, do something good. I don't want you to have to watch your sons go to war because we couldn't fix it."

"Joseph...? It sounds like your saying more, something that isn't just your allegiance to me."

"I'm saying goodbye Perttu. I love you as a brother, I will die for you, I will endure anything for your children and I'm saying that I do this for you! That I will do whatever you want of me in this moment. I will unleash the magic in me for the good. But that is the last thing I will do. I'll make sure Thomas and Aurora and Philip and Jack have a life of relative peace but then I do not want to walk the world anymore. I have fought for so long; I have seen things that make sleeping hard to do. I can not do it any longer. I'm sorry... I'm so sorry."

"Joseph! Joseph where are you going?! Come back. You can't! Don't you walk away from me! Don't you tell me that, I need you! Joseph! Think of the children, they love you. Don't walk away..! Joseph..."

"I've made my mind up; I'll see you at the end of the week. Then we can finish this business."

Chapter 16

It was hard to know that the world was a little lonelier. His family had joined him and Perttu had told Lily of Joseph's decision. The children played with the sorcerers and were loving the tricks they did which tended to involve flowers and magic. Perttu could relax. He didn't want to think about the week's end, when everything would slowly come to an end.

"Lily, go home. Take the kids."

"But-;"

"No Lily. You're still new to this world; I don't want you to see death. I don't want the children to see him and get attached and then ask me where uncle Joseph has gone. Please, let my father take you home."

"Fine!" She was angry at being dismissed like a weak child. "Fine, me and the children will go home... But Perttu, don't give up on him. Don't give up even at the last second. Minds change quicker than a rain drop, he is more than your cousin and he is more than an adopted brother, Perttu... Joseph is your brother, so don't fail him; even if he's on his way to failing you."

Her mother had organised the dress, the church, the flowers and the guests were all invited. The hall that was to hold the reception was booked and Elsa was throwing up without fail every morning. The marriage was set and while she knew she was doing the right thing for her family, and for this lovely man she called a true friend, as the days crept closer she felt an almighty wrenching in her belly that got worse and worse until she couldn't keep any food down. Alexander was no longer coming round as usual. News of her weak stomach was no doubt putting him off and she found herself obliged to write to him explaining that she would be better in a few days. That itself was a few days ago and there was no change to her sickness.

It felt as if her very body was weighing her down, causing her pain and convulsions in order to keep her from moving around, moving forward. She was wondering how she would manage to walk to the church in a few days' time when every day she sat in a chair huddling herself up into a small ball and taking small slow steps, only when necessary. Every time Joseph flashed as a memory in her mind she would have to hobble to privacy, very quickly, in order to be sick. He hadn't wrote to her or called on her and she was sure that his friend would have, by now, told him the news. She was glad she hadn't had to do it, just the thought of it made her feel so depressed she burst into floods of tears.

Her mother had sent for the doctor but he had no real idea what was wrong with her. He had bled her arm and prepared her foul medicine that didn't work, but other than that all he really did was sigh and mumble incoherently as he pottered about humming to himself. She wasn't cured and she wasn't even on her way to being together. She hoped it would fade by her wedding; she couldn't walk down the aisle with a bucket in her hands just in case she was sick. It would be called off if she was too ill and she panicked at the stir that would cause. The people would gossip like crazy if she had to cancel. Cancelling would let down Alexander and she didn't want to have to see his face if she did. She expected that it would look sad with a hint of anger in it because she was making him look a fool. Her mother would never let her hear the end of it and she would be lucky if all her father did was rage at her for a full day and night. It wasn't an option she wanted to consider (cancelling) but after she was cleaning herself up, after a nasty bout of sickness, she recognised that it was one she had no choice but to contemplate. She needed to make alternate arrangements if that were the case and she needed to tell the vicar, and hall owner, that the dates would be changing. For they would never be cancelled, not now. But it could be moved to a later date. A slight inconvenience to everyone but not a scandal. Nothing too major.

One of the servants brought her some stew and bread but the smell immediately sent her stomach churning. Rushing off to relief her convulsing stomach she closed her eyes and let her legs turn to jelly. The floor was soon covered in a mess and she still didn't try to move away. Knelt on the ground her hands steadied her body so she didn't fall down onto the sick in front of her and in that moment – the lowest of all her life she understood that she was doing this to herself. That this illness was caused by her because she made the wrong choice; this was her punishment. With tears streaming down her face she screamed her lungs out when a servant tried to get her up. The minute someone stooped down to lift her up she kicked out, threw her hands all around the air and cried and cried. She didn't want anyone to pick her up; she deserved to be on the floor, she deserved to be positioned in a state of grovelling and she didn't want anyone to pick her up – that was for her to do, it was her responsibility to sort out the mess she was in and she screamed that out loud for all the house to hear. Decorum was gone, modesty was gone, every tiny speck of etiquette training was gone and all that mattered now was that they left her alone to figure out her life.

Hands left her and she stopped making a fuss instead she watched as the servant hurried out of the room and then she understood that the doorbell had rang. Glad for the silence she huddled up and cried some more.

The enchantress had got the date of the next battle and Joseph was busy meditating. Apparently Jaol said it helped but so far Jaol insisted Joseph was doing it wrong anyway.

"What's wrong with you lad? You can lift the sea with your mind but you can't relax it and block the world out for a single minute?! Do it again."

Secretly Joseph loved being pushed, he liked getting frustrated and he like knowing he couldn't get to the count of three before a thought entered his mind. He began to realise he was overthinking things - big style. The aim was to count for as possible, if anything else, anything at all, came into his head that wasn't the next number, then he had to start again from number one. Eventually the idea was that he wouldn't concentrate as much on the numbers and the end goal was to close his eyes and not think of anything, not even numbers. The point was to experience a sense of nothingness. It was weird but he was trying, and failing terribly but he found the more he got angry at the meditation and at the process, the more he concentrated only on this new concept called mediation and less on Elsa. That he was very grateful for.

The enchantress walked in white, bare footed against the garish green. Her slender legs were tall, her body just as elongated and even her hair fell lengthways to the middle of her back. Everything about her was designed to be alluring, beautiful and delicate. But inside of her there was a core of steel. She kept herself hidden as best as she could and she wielded her magic as and when needed. She could do terrible things, just as Joseph could do, but she could do it best to those who fell under her spell of beauty. Joseph had never fallen under that spell of her looks and so could not manipulate his mind, but others she could. Men mostly. She knew his pain and apprehension about using power but she had grown to understand exactly when it was needed.

Walking away from her prey she glanced once more back at the man dressed in dirty brown clothes. He had been walking for days to get to her and she had mercilessly extracted from his mind information about the next battle, the big battle, not some small one, and she had used him to plant the seed that this battle was needed. Her work had been going on for months. And now it would end.

Her forests were being destroyed, her people were scattering, all for the politics of a species she wasn't even a part of. It angered her and when she had gained the information she needed she was so appalled at it that she had killed her informant. He was useless anyway now, he had done his job, his purpose, and now he was a liability; she couldn't guarantee the safety of her or her kind when he wasn't submerged under layers of hypnotic power.

"You killed him."

Turning slowly she looked back towards Niklas.

"Sometimes, even I cannot always control my powers."

"You sent him mad."

"He died happy; they always do when they look upon me."

"You need a lesson in control."

"I need my people safe, Niklas. I need my forests back. I need Perttu to reign in his cousin and I need Joseph to get over his mate."

"Get over? Get over? How? That is his Bride, his only chance of happiness in a world of death and hatred. In a world plagued with memories he can't handle she was his chance of sanity! Get over?!..."

"I'm Sorry!"

She screamed it at him and her strong demeanour seemed to falter. Then she fell to her knees while tears poured down her face.

"I wanted him to stop the vampires from fighting; they will create another hell on this earth if they are allowed to continue. I wanted Joseph to go in peacefully and be diplomatic... but look at him, he can't."

She turned around and looked at Niklas with frowning eyebrows and her lips turned into a regretful expression of disdain. "I needed him to come through! I want my home back! I tried to use my beauty but it didn't work. Do you know how exhausting it is to convince someone without power? He is stubborn and right now he is only just in control."

"What are you saying?"

"His kind have taken my home and their war has killed my kin! I was going to let them have the easy way out and I was going to train him in order to gain attention and stop this needless fighting. I was even going to put power in the hands of Joseph and Perttu together. But now I don't know what to do! I can kill a man easily Niklas but I don't want to. I can't see what is the best course of action here and

I'm scared that I'm going to lose everything because I put so much trust in one person. What if he loses control like he told me he was afraid of?! He begged me to leave him alone and I told him we could protect everyone from his destructive nature. And now, now I don't think I can reign him in and I'm scared about what disaster he can create if I let him loose."

Niklas felt as if he was on a seesaw and constantly unbalanced. He didn't know what was what anymore. The enchantress did not loss control, she didn't cry or kill and she certainly didn't ever show that she was indecisive to the point of despair.

"What are you really saying? They are covering more land I know it, I see it day by day the mess they leave behind at the battle sites but why does that affect you, you can always move on to another forest can't you?"

"I can't! Don't you see that every creation is given a power but they are also given a weakness! You sorcerers are given power but you pay for it by tiring. Vampires are given an immortal body, a weapon to be wielded, but they are bound by moonlight and cannot stand the sun. I am a forest dweller, as are my kin. I fled from one forest Niklas and it hurt. It tore me up inside to leave a home and I had no beauty when I got here. By nature my beauty everything I am, depends on the surroundings. If a forest is lush, I am also. If the forest thrives then so do I. I am the forest, it gives life to me and I give it back. If the war stretches to my home I will die Niklas. My kin will die. I want it over. I want to sleep at night and know I'll live to the next. I am scared!"

Niklas walked over to her and feeling as though he might be overstepping his position he decided everyone needed a hug at some point. He knelt down beside her and wrapped his arms around her.

"You toying with a lot of ideas are you? You want Joseph to come through but you still feel the need to have a backup in case he doesn't. You're thinking of doing bad things aren't you? Of taking charge of the situation as your own powers would allow you to do?"

"I could kill him if I didn't hate myself so much for even thinking that."

"Then take that as good omen. You're holding on for him My Lady, you're still being strong. Show him that, let him prove himself to us. Don't abandon him now."

"I've disgraced myself haven't I?"

"Of course you haven't, we've all wavered at some point with this plan. That you're on your knees crying proves you still care enough about a peaceful outcome, so come on, let's get you on your feet and all elegant again." He smiled at her and she playfully hit him on the arm.

"I'm always elegant."

Niklas helped her to her feet and cast a glance at the one she had killed. "I don't want to mess with you any time soon."

"I shouldn't have done that."

"Learn from your mistake as you keep trying to get Joseph to do. What information did the informant give you?"

"There is a battle in two days."

"Let's go tell everyone then."

Joseph was quite relieved when they told him the date had been set. He stopped meditating at once deciding a swim would be better for preparation. He noticed the enchantress' wary eyes and frowned but in the end left her. He had some thinking to do.

And so the night whiled away and he slept the following day. The next night appeared and he spent it lying on the ground looking up at the black sky and counting the stars, to wait out the calm before the storm. The sun began to come up and he went to sleep and then he woke up on the second night... the night of battle.

The day dawned and he awoke to the serene face of the enchantress looking at him.

"Morning." He greeted her.

"Good morning, Joseph. I have made you your suit; I hope it's to your liking."

"You look sad."

"I almost lost my faith in you Joseph. I nearly did something terrible..."

"We've all done terrible things. At least you only considered doing yours. I haven't exactly set a good example for you all have I?"

He motioned for her to turn around while he got himself dressed, he felt numb. As if he wasn't a person anymore. Emotion was out of the window. It had to be. "I won't let you down."

"I'll leave you to get dressed."

She left him to it and he looked at what she had brought him to wear. He was shocked, it was all white. White? Of all the colours, he was going to go onto a bloody and dirty battlefield dressed in white. He shook his head; well if she wanted a statement then let there be a statement. He stripped his clothes off, washed himself in the water he had collected the day before, and then began the layering of clothes. His crisp white shirt looked to have been ironed straight but he knew her magic would have created it in such a pristine condition. He pulled on his trousers, buttoning the waistline button and attaching his braces. There wasn't an inch that wasn't white; there wasn't even a speck of grey dust on them.

He picked up his cravat and made sure to put it on as neatly as possible and then he slipped on the waistcoat. Already he felt too enclosed, it was as though with the layers of clothing he was slowly disappearing to the material. Still he wasn't done. A white jacket came next and he found that a silver pocket watch lay beside a silver topped cane. His shoes were all white and he felt a little silly. She meant it as a message of purity. Of innocent. But he was far from innocent.

His black hair was out of place now but he shrugged it off. If it came to it in battle he was sure to destroy the clothes he was wearing to protect his friends....

.... Protect his friends. The image of Jaol and Niklas and even the enchantress was in mind... he felt something for them. He felt as if he really couldn't bear to see them die in this battle. And it surprised him. Their images were the things that pushed through his grief-stricken numbness. And the children. Lily and Perttu had come and their involvement would squeeze his heart but if the children... if the children saw hell, it would shatter him from the inside.

He put a hand to his heart and behind his eyes, visions he didn't know had wills of their own portrayed in his mind the figures of the enchantress' kin. Their slender, feminine and graceful yet strong bodies were no match for the knives that were the vampire's bodies. The other sorcerer's, the men whose gnarled fingers told him of years of hard work, had seen too much already to have to go into battle again. He felt his breathing escalate. He had always fought for others, that was what he had been brought up to do and yet in the face of everything he had nearly forgotten why he had lived for so long. Why he had endured the white days only to still wage war at the end of them... He was a man with a heart. He truly did want peace and right now he was thinking that he would lay down his life for any of his family, or his 'holders'; though even they had become good friend by now.

He would always know sorrow at never having a mate but at least he had those who cared for him and him for them. He had something. And he wouldn't see them lost!

Closing the top button to his shirt he didn't feel suffocated anymore, he didn't feel as though the button took his breath away; he felt dignified. He felt as if he was making a stand against the tyrants of his own race. He felt as if he could do something important and to that he needed to make an important effect with correct attire. He fastened the pocket watch to the inside of his waistcoat and slipped the round clock into the outside top pocket on his left. He found white gloves and he took the time to put them on precisely so the seams matched the sides of his fingers, and then he picked up the cane and held on to it while he straightened his back and lifted up his head. He wouldn't fail his friends and family. He needed to show them his changed expression, he didn't want to stand there on the battle field with his own people wondering if he'll lose his head or not.

Stepping out from his little spot in the forest he was greeted by everyone in a semi-circle waiting for him.

"Morning." He said looking for a familiar face. He saw Perttu on his right and Niklas was off to his left. "I just want you all to know that I won't lose it. I've had time to put things in perspective." He explained what it was that had changed and then turned away from them all until they couldn't see his expression. He didn't want to get too emotional with them. It was dangerous, yes. They could lose their lives if things got out of hand but he still didn't want to the weepy eyed, gushing swords things.

Unbeknown to him Niklas had picked up the hand of the enchantress and was nodded encouragement to her.

"You see My Lady, trust him." The words were spoken so quietly Joseph didn't hear them but the enchantress didn't look so scared anymore.

Joseph started to walk in the direction of the battle, following the enchantress who had taken lead. Around him her kin walked, they enclosed him in a circle of their grace and he felt heavy footed and clumsy in comparison to them but he had to get over that. They were strange creatures these forest dwelling enchanters. Behind them came the sorcerers and lastly came Perttu who was walking with a prowl to his step. Perttu wanted to make sure their procession had no spies of surprise attacks. He felt proud, did Perttu, he felt as if he was watching the debut of a younger brother; finally he saw that Joseph was going to do something great, something extraordinary that would make sure his name would never be forgotten, no matter the outcome. And he was proud that Joseph had trained so hard, confronted his demons and even got over the loss of a mate to do the right thing. The last one was the biggest achievement. Perspective was hard to get sometimes.

Joseph felt the tension in the air when they were getting closer and he stopped abruptly. Blundering in would do no good at all. "Surround the battlefield; I will walk into it on my own." He said, every nodded and made their way left and right in order to filter around the fighting. Joseph did this on purpose, he wanted them out the danger zone and the outskirts were the best option. Feeling overcome with energy he doubled over for a second. Since noticing his own strength and the power that ran through his veins he tended to feel it around him now. As if it was prodding him all the time waiting for him to take it and manipulate it as he wished. It was as if he could use it right from the air and it didn't matter if it was running in his body or alongside it as long as magic was there.

He gripped his stomach as it bombarded him. There was so many fighting here, all using powers of their own sorts that it was like an on slaughter to him to feel all the magic static around him. He breathed deeply, with every breath he allowed himself to feel the crackle of energy around him and draw it inside of him, to build up in his own self, in his veins and in his blood vessels. He could feel himself feeling strangely full inside. As if he had drank too much blood, it nourished him. He kept his eyes closed as it dawned on him that he was using the residue that was left by others using their power. This battlefield, to him, was potentially a feast. He was getting stronger with every concentrated breath he took. No wonder he had been good in previous battle; despite the lack of training and using only minimal magic, he must have subconsciously been doing this for years and not noticing because he never delved deep into his own abilities.

He took a step forward and felt no ground under him. Surprised he looked down to find that he was floating, an inch from the ground he was stood and his white shoes and the bottoms of his trousers weren't getting dirty. An inch was rather inconspicuous and he smiled thinking that no would notice until he stopped walking, so he carried on floating.

Through the trees he led his own way, going straight and not deviating from the path. The sounds of war were loud in his ear and only getting louder. The feline screams of pain, rage and frustration filled his mind. The clicking of hair whipping around in the air, unsheathed like claws was chilling and he could hear the heavy thuds of bodies colliding in the air as they ran to beat each other. He heard piercing screams as vampires were torn apart and killed in seconds and he heard the jeering, the laughing the drooled mockery that came from mouths too dislocated to speak properly. Elongated teeth didn't leave for a human mouth.

The closer he got the more he could sense where things were around him. Every tree seemed to dent the aura of magic that was around him. It left him able to navigate his way through things without even needing to see where he was going and a twitch in the aura told him when to expect an object. It was as if the magic itself had shielded him and was on guard, telling him what he needed to know. So he thought he would try it out. He closed his eyes again. If this power was within him then he had get used to it at some point. He had to trust it, as it no doubt trusted him since the magic had developed within him all those years ago.

With a single breath he merged with it, fell in line with it and suddenly restraint was nothing. It was as if it was another limb to him, it was a part of him so explicitly that he needed just to tap it with his mind and it would stop short of what it was doing. Why now, all of a sudden, was he doing easily what had taken so long of training and practising to just to live with and utilise? Now he couldn't understand why it had taken so long to 'feel' it.

He walked into the clearing with his eyes closed, his clothes white and altogether radiant and clean and his feet not even touching the floor. A nudge by his head told him to tilt and he did. He did not see the vampires that flew overhead, each having launched into each other, but he felt the wind ruffle his hair as they did. He had a soft yet unmovable grip on the cane, it was actually little comforting to him to have that - though he didn't really know why. He altered his course by a few inches when the aura flickered a little at his feet and again, he did not need to see it, to know he had avoided a fallen vampire.

The stench of blood and innards was strong but he commanded the aura to shift and block his nose and that it did within a second of thinking about it. He did not need to open his eyes to know that he hadn't gained attention until he came to the middle of the clearing, right in the middle of the battle where enemy or comrade was a mystery and everything was one big chaotic mess of limb, hair and weapon. The silence came as abruptly as his appearance to them had been. It instantly quietened. The battle seeming to stop for a brief reprieve and it was only when he felt the eyes of every one of his fellow vampires did he open his eyes and look out at them all, appalled.

"What are we doing?"

Chapter 17

"What are we doing?" He said to them. "Why are we killing our own kin?"

No one answered him and he frowned at them all. "Does no one remember the white days? Does no one here understand what will happen if this is not sorted out now?! Do you all want to die?!"

His cry seemed to reach deaf ears as they stared at him and his insolence. Until one came forward, one with whom he had fought alongside on many occasions. "Joseph? I thought you were united in this? I thought you knew what we were doing. We're fighting for freedom, our kin would take that from us if we did not fight back."

"Then the question is why are our kin trying to take it from us?" His calm manner was startling everyone and he was sure he had their attention only because of their shock.

"We take if from you because we can be so much more than we are. If we do as our king says and you follow our lead then we can come out in the open without having to be afraid of the humans. We can be strong and we can be united as one!" A vampire he had seen at many of his battles, as his enemy, spoke out to him.

"Why are we not united already? We each have our clans, our leaders but together we form one, we rule ourselves and no one is left behind. We speak our minds to our fellow kin and no one rules over the other inexplicably."

"But that doesn't happen!" The vampire cried out and thrust his hands at Joseph, the claws nails almost tearing at his waistcoat but Joseph caught the vampires wrists... and the vampire froze for a second. The hairs on his arms were sticking up and yet Joseph wasn't cut. The vampire wondered what magic it was that pushed the blades rather than have them injure but then it didn't matter to the vampire anymore, he wanted to explain why he was so angry. "Some of us have spoken for years about how we don't want isolation and still we have to live in fear from our very food source! Other vampires in clans that offer freedom overlook us that are forced to remain hidden in caves and wilderness!"

"Then that is a failing that should be address, solved, not fought over!"

"Nothing changes with voice alone!" Another vampire spat the words at Joseph and the one whose wrists he had hold of, suddenly pulled free.

The façade was gone. The surprise element of his control magic was lost on them and all at once they lunged for him; and each other. Naked bodies of pure weapon leap to him and he knew now he didn't even have to move his hovering feet. He simply sighed and they stopped mid-air, their poses – of leaping in the air – were captured like a photograph. With bent knees and exposed bellies they now hovered in front of Joseph, high in the air.

"I do not want to see another age of white days. Those hideous times are behind us. They need to be behind us." He said simply.

"We don't care about the white days!"

"We want to fight today!"

"I don't even remember those times!"

"It would be an honour to return to them and fight for what we believe in!"

And so they all began shouting at him but that last comment pushed his patience too far. He was losing control again.

"Honour." He whispered it softly to himself. "Honour! Honour you say?!" He screamed it, pushed with all his force those he held in the air and watched as he sent them flying backwards to land in heaps on the floor. "How dare you speak of what you do not know! How dare you say the word honour when talking of that time! How dare you."

He reached out a hand, palm upwards and with everyone's captivated attention, he slowly brought his finger inwards to form a fist and the young vampire who dared to speak of honour came toward him. Dragged by magic along the floor, along the blood and the mud and bodies the young vampire screamed at the indignity and then again when his mouth was covered in mess from the floor. No amount of struggling would stop him from being dragged towards Joseph though, he would be taught a lesson now.

Joseph let the boy come right up to his feet before he lifted him to his eye line so the lad's full body was in the air. He wanted the young one to have no control over his body. None what so ever. So he toyed with him, revolving him around in a circle twice, just to put more fear into the boys head. "Honour. Do you feel honour at the moment?" He gave the boy a smile, it wasn't a menacing one, it was patronising, a knowing one. And a little mocking. "You feel like a big brave solider dying for your belief?"

The young vampire looked terrified. "Answer me."

"No."

"No. Of course you don't. Do you think when I was forced to lay in the sun, too weak to move, and endured the searing pain of my flesh being cooked, that I felt honour then?"

Everyone was at a standstill, he could feel his aura shaking and knew it was the boy who trembled and knocked it with every jerk.

"No."

"There is no honour is fighting and dying, there is no honour in slaying one's kin. And it has taken a while for me to understand that." He softened his voice a little and looked at them all. "I ask that you all understand that now; before it's too late. Before we descend back into the days of traitorous hell once more." He put the vampire back on the floor and nodded at him to fall back into the ranks that stood behind him. The vampire scurried off waiting orders and yet hesitant to join back with those that went against Joseph.

... Silence. Until;

"We won't stop. We can't stop. Our king wants us to win and you and your side don't want us to. There is no compromise to be made here today."

"Surprisingly you sound sad." Joseph noticed that the speaker even looked a little repentant.

"We signed up for this, we will see white days if we must."

He felt a little sorrow at the answer but wondered as well why they had no charged him yet. Where they already under a rule too strict to back out from? This King of theirs, he wondered where he was. It seemed as if they were not going to see sense, that they were not going to understand what it was they were leading up towards and he was scared that he had no power over them. "Then let me show you, in detail, what will happen next." A last bid attempt to turn them from their King.

Where he got the power and how he instinctively knew what he could do with it, he would never know but he brought his hands together, palms facing each other and slowly he separated them while in the space between them there, slowly emerged, an image. It depicted the day he fought, a memory straight from his mind; he was projecting it outwards and slowly he let his hands part more and more, lifting them up higher and higher until above his head. His whole arms were separated and then he pushed the image outwards – he pushed it onto them, so they were enveloped in it, like snow in a child snow globe they were trapped inside a dome. "Let me show you." He said again.

Thrown into an illusion everyone on the battle field saw, as if with their very own eyes, the sun. And it was blinding. Standing on sand they felt, though distantly, the pain of coarse pebbles on the soles of their feet and stuck to hair follicles and wounds. They felt the burn of the sun and they saw its rays from the distance. The rising sun in the desert was both beautiful and destructive. They feared it, coward from the image of it but they were stuck there, stuck in his memory of those days as if they were actually there, feeling its burn and not able to do anything. Slowly he forced them to look down at the sand and he heard the gasps as they saw what it was that haunted him at night.

Sand should have been yellow, even back in the days were records of things weren't kept. The sand however, was red. And all around were the bodies of vampires. It did not look rewarding, it did not look like victory... it looked... so sad. Each face was back to its human self, they had chosen to die as men rather than animals, with their dying wish they wanted to look at peace even if they had lived like barbarians in the end. And each face had its eyes closed, their eyelashes looked delicate on their pale skin. So many lips were parted in death and they looked like lovers about to kiss and yet all they had done when they were alive was part them to scream and shout and jeer. The irony of their images only broke Joseph's heart and it was something he got across to them in his memory.

He showed them then what he had to do but with a twist. They lived it, so as if they themselves were burning in the sun they seemed to drag themselves out of its rays, through the blood and the bodies and the sand that stuck to them with each inch they crawled. They got to caves and were lost in the memory of Joseph coating his body in wax and peeling it off, taking his hair with it... and the sand and the dead flesh that had rotted under the sun's beams. The memory of that pain was not one he dulled for them. He let them feel the excruciating pain, he let them see how he recovered during the day only to wake and fight once more at night. They watched him again and again slit throat and bodies parts until it was automatic to fight someone to the death. He introduced him to a life were killing had become so normal it was part of the routine that was 'losing himself in the battle'. So that the pain he went through each day of waxing and healing was nothing to the mental torture he went through. Every scream he memorized, every wound he had inflicted he logged.

They watched as he became powerful and still had to scrap the floor with his hand and knees to survive. They watched as he lived through it slowly forgetting the point of the wars in the first place, and until he craved the darkness and the grim setting of what was his home back in England. They saw that when he closed his eyes at night he wished for water, not blood, and that over time the same sights every night and day were boring holes into his mind that scarred him and hurt. They gasped when they saw he longed for humanity to creep back into his world again.

"Now you know what will come if we cannot sort this amongst ourselves. Maybe then you will stop this madness."

"We are not responsible for your memories – your wars and your silly desires for it to stop. We are not responsible for that!"

A vampire came striding forward when Joseph's hands were by his side again and he regarded the vampire with distaste. The vampire was smirking at him evilly. "Some of us have a king we wish to serve; we won't stop doing his bidding because one vampire decided he didn't want to fight anymore. His conscience was too fragile."

Joseph did not like this vampire.

"Can you not see that he is trying to rid the vampire world of its weakest so there is more food for those who survive? Can you not see the destruction, this king you would bow down to, is doing? He does not care about you, he sends you to battle again and again. Brothers of each side why are we doing this? Why are we turning on each other! We have lived peacefully for years, we have mingled amongst the mortal kind and nothing bad has happened, why not stay in our communities and rule as a partnership between families? If you really want a king, if you desire one true leader, why are you kneeling to a king who is sending to you war with no mercy? Where is your king if this cause is so important to him?"

"He offers us power! Those who fight for him will be high class vampires, we will rule over you weaker vampires. Let's kill the weak ones!" An insolent one yelled at Joseph before turning to the crowd around him, "If they don't know what is good for them, if they are not strong then they do not deserve to be a part of our new age!"

Frantically looking around Joseph tried yet again, "You would kill the mortals, you wish to make them a food source and nothing more. Do you really want to be the monsters they think we are?"

"Your side is not so worthy, they do not think well of the humans as you do Joseph. They are weak, fighting for fighting's sake."

"I could say the same about you. At there are those that do not fight to kill the humans. At least they fight for democracy, for the chance of a community amongst a race forced to live in secret. They fight your leadership and the rule of your king, they are free men and have the guts to die for that. They are not weak." He was so angry that this was being questioned.

"You cannot stop this." The same vampire said. "You cannot stop us from slaughtering your side."

"Do you know what will happen to you once you win? In years to come when you have fought so hard and your bodies are damaged, when your minds are shattered and you walk everyday on the verge of insanity, do you know what your king will do then?"

The vampire in front of him sad nothing, the smirk fell a tiny fraction and his eyes bore into Joseph's. "He will reorganise us so we are powerful vampires."

"He cannot give you magic. The man who sends you to your death will rule over you... if you survive. A man that merciless as your superior, my friend, will lead only to your own oppression; in the end."

He faltered. The smirking vampire faltered a little and everyone around was filled with dismay. Not only that, their eyes suddenly widened. "Our king will greet you now." 'Smirker' said but his strong voice had gone and Joseph got the impression that the vampire had just given him a warning.

Sure enough the ranks of vampires on either side parted way and left a path for the one that was supposed to be the new King. He too came dressed for the occasion.

In a purple trench coat the king walked forward, his human hair was blonde and his face looked angry. Joseph still couldn't fear him. It wasn't until the King got about a foot away from Joseph did he notice something bump his aura. But there was nothing that close to him. It bumped it again and his aura seemed to tingle a little. An ominous feeling began to settle in his very heart and then he worked it out.

"No, it can't be..."

"Pleased to meet you Joseph. I had wondered. I had wondered if those days had corrupted anyone else as they had me. The wars taught me one thing; only the strong survive Joseph. Join me, you are strong as well and I could use another equal, someone just like me, on my side."

Chapter 18

What doesn't kill you makes you stronger. That is the saying that so many told him over and over again but it didn't feel like he had got strong, it just felt as if another adversary had come his way.

"Strength doesn't get you everything. Strength can't rule a species!"

"It can. Join me Joseph, or I'll show you just what strength can do."

Confused at his opponent he turned around to look back at the enchantress by the trees. Had she known? Yes, she had; he saw it in her face – regret.

"I'm sorry Joseph. He's known me from many years back. He threatened my land personally and my kin. You were the only one I knew who could defeat him. I figured your race needed that lifeline as well."

Her soft voice carried across the field for she was sheltered amongst the woods. A bit of warning would have been nice. Maybe an inkling into what exactly he was up against and what she was doing but no, she had kept him in the dark. Well... he had come here with one job in mind and he wasn't going to turn away from it now. He figured the forest that had been his home for many weeks now, was too pretty to be destroyed anyway. He smiled at her and nodded once. "I'd best get to business then hadn't I?"

He visibly saw the relief on her face as he turned back to the kind. "You are from the white days yourself."

"Yes, I endured everything you endured until I was carried away by a stranger and healed in the darkness of a cave until the war ended."

"Interesting. I saw that war end. I was in it when the sun burnt through the remaining ranks and cremated the leaders on either side."

The king curled his lip but Joseph merely carried on, a new expression on his face. Could it be pride? "I guess I was strong one then, I held out longer than you in that battle." He couldn't help a little taunt toward the arrogant king. "I won't join you. I'll take you away so there is no chance of your rule and then we can go back how we were living before. Only once you're gone I'll make sure some changes happen; I'll make sure those who hadn't had a voice before, will have one now. We should all learn from our mistakes."

He looked back at the vampire that had first talked to him about why he joined forced under the kings rule and with eye contact he promised the vampire, change. So wrapped was Joseph in trying to promise a difference that he didn't see the blow, his aura dented suddenly and a pressure hit him low in his stomach taking the air from his lungs and sending him rocking backwards on his feet. Staggering a little from the unprepared blow he ground his teeth and dug the heels of his feet into his aura to anchor himself and stop himself from falling back. He closed his eyes for a second.

No matter how much diplomacy he tried for or whether he wore a suit or not, battle today was inevitable. "So it begins." He said but he wouldn't let anyone else join in either. Too much devastation had already occurred for that.

With a glance around at the vampires he expanded his magic to create a border to keep everyone back from him and the king and then he forced each vampire still. He tied them to the spot they stood and he heard their gasps as he locked them in their crouched or standing positions, made to watch but not take part, and then he lifted up his hands, palms upwards and rose a little more off the ground. "I don't want to dirty this suit." He explained as he waited for the next blow with his eyes piercing the kings. Let it end now. Let everything end now. He had a bad feeling that unleashing his power like this was going to feel rather good...

He thrust out power only for the king to do the same and in the middle of them was a fight of forces. Joseph, leading with his little finger, made an arc raising his fingers and lowered them. The stones around them both lifted from the ground, into the air and began to revolve around both of them. He made them encase the fighting pair in a circle, yet ready at any moment to pelt forward in attack or form a wall of defence should he need it. He blinked and tried to attach magic to the king ankles, to drag him down, but the king was ready for that and he pushed out a bolt of magic that hit Joseph in the face. He wasn't fazed. Bringing his fingers to his thumb he spread them out, like signing that a flower was blooming, and his nails unsheathed into claws, the pointed nail exuding sparks of magic. Dragging them down the air in a scratching motion he magically ripped five wounds into the kings chest, an aura was not a shield. They were still about five feet apart yet the roar from the king as his blood started to run down his chest was so loud they may as well have been stood face to face.

Taking a stance, with his back leg bent as leverage the King was beyond angry now. Riled to a new intensity he cried out to the sky and brought the magic up from his toes and through his body, until he pushed out magic from inside of his very chest and through his hands. A loud crackling and bang was heard, like thunder and static mixed together. Joseph was ready for this, like a gunshot the magic hurtled towards him, about to blow him backwards at the least. He stood his ground, raising his hands he remembered the training with the arrows. To stop it without throwing it back, ultimate control – he smiled. This was training put into practise and as the blow of power flew to his body he raised both hands and tried to take the overspill into him, to use it as a counter balance to the heavy force of magic.

He stopped it – the bomb of magic and watched as a mirage looking substance halted inches from his body. He could see the magic for the first time and he smiled at how incredibly fragile it looked, but how powerful it really was. Then he noticed that it wasn't the magic that was powerful, it was the leverage behind it that controlled the weight and destruction (or protection) of that fragile force.

He tried to understand it some more, to get his head around the subject that was magic and wielding it but at that moment another burst of magic came at him and while he stopped it with his right hand, another blow at his left hurtled close to his face, shearing off a layer of flesh at his cheek and stinging, his hair rippled as the magic pushed past it... but he never moved an inch. He made to fight back but his aura suddenly felt disfigured, squeezed, as if a weight was converging in on it and trying to pop it like a balloon. With inner strength Joseph tried to fight it, he found his own stomach clenching as he tried to project the awareness of magic, that was his aura, back around him. It was hard and he felt his breath stick in his lungs at the effort this cause until he decided defence wasn't going to work.

Gathering more magic in his hands her tried to understand everything he needed. Not the power but the wielder. It flowed within him but he contained it. He freed it when he pleased, he holed as he wanted to. It was a tool. It was nothing more than the hairs on his arms; as deadly as they were inactive when pushed flat.

Understanding only made it easier to use. He breathed deep, taking the excess power inside of himself, absorbing it, to use later. The he gathered those sparks on his nail tips again and flicked them, one by one, at the king's aura. He dented it again and again and again, forcing the king to repair his own awareness with every second that went by and when the king was preoccupied with his aura, Joseph took a step forward and crushed the king's aura using his whole body as a weight with which to push out his magic. Then he brought down rain, only on the king, from the cloud directly above he drained it dry so the water drenched the king and made his long purple coat limp. Joseph laughed. "See how silly this fighting is?"

Swiping his wet hair in the air, the king brought a swift retaliation by slicing at Joseph's face so the blood slid down the stubble on his cheek. Joseph swiped his arms from high left to low right and hurtled magic back, he pushing so the king was unbalanced until he gave one final push forwards. The king however did not fall and Joseph brought his right hand up, curling it into a fist as he gathered energy into his palm. Taking a steps forward he released his hand and threw magic at the king. He kept up a constant stream of bombardment as he walked forward, each hand producing ammunition and getting closer to the king. He hoped to knock him down but the king was withstanding the assault and was even erecting a shield at the same time.

Joseph didn't see it; maybe he was distracted, maybe just inexperienced. Or just maybe, he wasn't good enough to multi-task. Snaking across the floor had been the Kings own magic and it was too late now for Joseph to stop it. For, coiled around his ankles was what looked like smoke but had the grip of a lions incisors; it bit into him. The smoke was insubstantial and oblivious to the hairs on Joseph's body. As it held him tightly in its unbreakable grip, he felt it inching further up his body. Like a cat clawing up a tree, the smoke edged up his legs breaking his skin and bleeding him.

"You are but an inexperienced child with your power, joseph." The king mocked him.

"But power is endurance, and I can still beat you even with my body being cut up."

Enough was enough now. A greater fight was needed. Narrowing his eyes Joseph ignored the pain and concentrated on his enemy, "I'll stop being nice now." He said finally and slowly he edged out his fingers spreading them wide so his long digits elongated and separated all the while channelling his magic towards the king. A thousands knife pricks hit the king in the chest and the more Joseph spread his hands the more they followed his movements, ripping through flesh and breaking the king as he was breaking Joseph. Breathing deep he forced the wind to rattle his hair and loosen it and he then he shook his head, allowing the clawed strands to click together but as they did sparks were emitted. He was directing his power out through every blade his body had.

Unperturbed by the smoke still tearing at his skin, he let himself hover from the ground even higher. His suit that was now ripped and bloody with his own blood still sheathed the knives that was his body hair but he smirked a little. He didn't even need his body anymore. Whipping his hair across he forced magic across to the king and as if whipped by his very hair the king bore magic welted gashes across his cheek.

"You will pay for this!" He screamed at joseph as he touched the crimson drops, "I will make you cry in agony and bow to me in disgrace when I have finished breaking your body!"

The king pulled his hands into fists and Joseph felt as if string had wrapped around his torso and was pulling him inwards. His breath caught inside of him and it hurt to expand his chest. The smoke was still trying to weigh him down and was slowly gaining more weight, trying to force him to the very floor. So used to pain, Joseph grit his teeth and brought his magic around him in a sort of bubble while he struggled to keep himself in his upright position in the air. This time though he let his teeth grow; his anger was hard to reign in now and the beast that was his natural vampiric state was forcing itself out of his human illusion. His jaw dislocated and his own incisors sank downwards past his lower lips. A growl bubbled up from his chest and he let out his own howl of defiance against his bonds.

The clouds were hiding the moon and he opened his eyes, pushing the clouds away with but a little thought to them. He wanted the light to shine down. He was annoyed that he was feeling so tied up and when the king's magic forced his arms out so he looked like he was tied to an ancient execution cross, he hissed in pure hatred and closed his eyes. It would take all the concentration he owned to accomplish what was on his mind right now but he vowed to do it anyway. He would do whatever it took to take this king down, to take away the threat of the world.

"Come to me." He said. "Come to me."

He sent his distorted voice into the night and with it he put in a compelling note. He sent it high into the sky and he called on the birds, the beetles, the ants, the spiders, the squirrels, the badgers and many more animals that lived in the forests. He let his magic twist and turn his words into an order that held desire, encouragement and no chance to ignore. He sent it to the animals and he waited for them to come to him and when they did he watched as they did their worse to the king. The insects that crawled started up his legs and they tickled him as they irritated his harsh skin. The squirrels threw nuts and berries at the king and the red/purple of berry juice stained the King's attire. The birds were worse they flew down and pecked at him, tried to draw his blood as he was doing to Joseph.

"This is me, being nice. This is me irritating you. Try and outsmart me now and I will let loose more than you can imagine."

"Using animals is a cowards way out!" The king spat as spiders bit him and badgers clawed his legs. The horde of wild animals now weighed the king down. "You deserve my mockery for that weak move."

"Try me." Joseph challenged him, urging him to be the worse he could be, so that Joseph could retaliate as the worse he too could be. "You just try it."

"With pleasure."

The king laughed and the magic around Joseph's chest tightened further until he was holding his breath to stop the pain of trying to take a breath. The smoke didn't just dig into his skin, it pierced it through until holes riddled his legs hips and were only getting higher with every second he let the kings magic get hold of him. Arrows, darts of power hurtled towards Joseph's face and he stopped them inches from his eyes, letting them fall to the ground. The King laughed as he ripped at Joseph's hair and watched as Joseph stood stoically enduring the torture. He went for Joseph's teeth, pulling at the incisors but this time Joseph merely shook his head in annoyance to rid himself of that weak power than tried to hurt him.

Now Joseph understood just how strong he was. While his body was battered with tiny bullets of force he took every one of the insults; he bore the magic and smiled at the bruises he was receiving but he did nothing. He was waiting for the right moment. The moment when he had absorbed enough magic to make what he was going to do next the final blow to end this battle. All the while he own flesh was being battered, he smirked.

"You know, I lost my Bride. I am alone in the world in regards a constant companion. I have family but I can never forget my past. It haunts me."

"You point?" The kind was openly laughing by now, thinking him winning Joseph.

"I walked into this knowing I would do anything to protect the ones I will no doubt leave behind."

Screams of denial behind were hard on his ears. He didn't want to hurt those who had trained him but he had truly seen enough of the wars and he was tired of everything, he did not mind this way. It was the only way anyway. "I can win you." He told the King, with a sad smile on his face now. "But I know that to do that is to push myself to limits that will break me, and I know that I stand in the way of everything I want to do. So let me show you what war really means."

The smile on the kings face fell, it was replaced with a wary confusion that was combined with such wide eyes that Joseph knew was more than apprehension. Pushing back every animal around him, including the vampires, he made them retreat a lot further back, pushing with his magic until he could no longer make out individual facial expressions. He pushed out the magic from body to enforce the shield around them, letting it shield layer up, again and again, thicker and stronger with each magic layer to ensure they were protected from everything. He made it so nothing could penetrate his shield and they could not leave it.

"I'm tired of seeing the innocent die." He said to the king. "So I'll use every inch of my energy store to save them."

He took a deep breath and stopped himself from gasping as the smoky claws stabbed a hole right in the middle of his belly. He closed his eyes for a second as blood poured from the wound. He had limited time until he would die now. He started by lifting the trees, he pulled about thirty up from the floor, roots and all and he saw the earth break and crumble, giving way as he ripped up the roots that lay under it. He pulled upwards bringing with them every stone, rock and boulder around.

"I did this when I grieved. I nearly hurt my friends by doing this." He informed the king. "This time it's controlled and this time it will be worse. You, my friend, will be my last kill. I swear it to the heavens, I shall not kill anymore after this... but then, I don't plan on being here anyway, to have that promise challenged." He chuckled humourlessly.

He felt that in the far distance there was a mountain. Not foolish enough to try ripping that up, since it was the very earth crusts itself and the devastation caused by that would be unbearable to those around, he hit out at the earth that made up the mountain and he assaulted the giant tower. He attacked the middle and upwards, hitting at its peak to break it up but only enough to separate the heavy rock from the lower part of the mountain. He wanted the majority of it to come to him. Bringing it down he literally tore down the mountain. Large boulders would have been pouring down the hillsides, falling into what lay beneath it, but he stopped them.

The whole top of the mountain was under his control, his power and he felt like he was doing the biggest press up known to man. He lifted the heavy weight of stone up and he pulled it towards him. Raised high into the sky was stone, tree and mountain and yet he decided it wasn't enough. He sucked in a breath and with it he brought some of the sea water with him. He didn't want the sea to run dry so he brought with him only a fraction its content. In the end, even the water was hovered high above the two of them and the king was staring in astonishment and terror as he understood what he was to be.

"My shield will protect them until I die but I have used enough that it will remain even longer afterwards. Maybe a few minutes after my death. I take you with me now, let our tormented and evil souls die together. We neither or us deserve to see the world anymore. We have both proved unreliable for that haven't we?"

He smiled as he saw his own death balanced above him. This was the end and what an end, he could finally be proud of himself now.

No more war. He had shown the fighters what would happen if they carried on, he had made sure each side of this knew why the other side fought against them and hopefully this would be the example that would end everything. The King who wanted corruption would be killed and the man who had killed so many would also fall into oblivion – showing them the lasting effect war had on people. It was hard to live with one's self after what they did in battle.

"Good bye." He said, letting go of the objects above them....

..... "Nooo!"

Chapter 19

Joseph hastily caught at floating death, the trees and the boulders and so on. Jolting them to a stop with wide eyes he turned to looked at Elsa. Not only was she on the battle ground but she had pierced his shield.

"How?" No, why had she done that? How had she got passed his own shield? "Elsa, get back!" He cried to her. The weight was hard on his insides, it was his own veins and tendons and ligaments that held the magic within him and those fine fibres inside his body held such a burden. A mountain of all things! "Elsa, get back."

"Don't do this, Joseph come back to me, please."

Was this a mirage? Was he back in the desert and so thirsty he was seeing things again? Her very hair seemed to be golden, like the sand before the blood fell. Her face was so... so smooth and beautiful he felt as if he was looking a precious stone; smoothed down to perfection. Her dress was fluttering in a light breeze that he was sure was due to the magic that swirled around the clearing.

But that was when he understood that he was not dreaming, this was no delusion brought on by a craving of sustenance, though he dearly needed some blood right at that moment. She was wearing a wedding dress and the lace that clung to the top of her body was delicious. Her pale skin underneath it was teasing him, even in the heat of battle he found her glorious to look at. But she wasn't his, she was a married woman now, bound by human law and he couldn't have her. He would not let her die though.

"Go back Elsa. Go back to your husband and have a happy life. Do not remember me. Go back."

"I left him! I didn't marry. Lilly came for me. Please don't do this."

"I have to. The King will do terrible things; even if he doesn't win the war he'll create a terrible age to come and I can't let my kin go through what I did. I can't do it Elsa."

"But now you know I am not taken you don't have to kill yourself, come to me, live!"

"I can't do that. I am tainted Elsa. And it's too late anyway, I cannot control these natural weapons I hold above my head unless I am outside the shield. They are heavy and even I have limitations; I can't slip inside the shield and hold them at the same time. One has to give."

"Then I'll die with you!"

His heart broke.

"No! Never!" He wouldn't be the cause of her death.

"Please Joseph, come to me."

He couldn't belift the words she was saying, she had refused to come to him when he needed her and now everything was planned out, she was here. She was hurting him by making him see everything he had longed for with a craving so bad he had done terrible things when he knew it would never be sated. And now he had gone too far, he could have it all but his actions had already denied it.

She stood watching him while her lungs gave out. Why had she not gone to him sooner. She was frozen to the spot, watching as he was giving himself up for this cause. She was losing him just as she had made him believe he had lost her. She deserved to see him die, she deserved that heartache but she didn't want it! "Joseph." She tried again, how foolish she had been. How ignorant she was of the atrocities of the world that she thought her father's disapproval the harshest reality she could live through. Never before had she thought herself selfish but at that moment she did. She felt as if she was blame for his hasty action.

The wedding dress felt dirty to her, it made her skin crawl to think it was designed for someone other than the man to whom she was a real Bride to. She hated the style of it, the thick skirt and tight bodice that screamed of the society she came from and the human restraints to which she had blindly conceded to. It rang out loud and clear her blinkered awareness of life. She had never considered another species of creature, let alone wars between them. She had never thought Joseph a man of so many emotions he struggled to contain them. And she paid dearly now for her childish view on life as she watched him shake with the strain of holding back his death... for her. So she could have her selfish last request.

"Please Joseph. Please."

"I can't. It's too late." Denying her what she pleaded with him for was heart shattering. To turn away from everything he wanted, to finish what he was doing was tearing up his insides more painfully than the king's smoky claws. So he appealed to the only people he knew could do what he couldn't.

As his Bride, his shield was open and closed to her at her will. He refused to kill her with himself so he looked to Perttu, his... his brother. And he looked at Niklas and the enchantress and then at Jaol. Combined they could create a shield for her as thick as his and it would cage her and protect her without her being able to resist.

"My brothers and sisters." He appealed to them. "Please, do this for I cannot."

They nodded and he watched as Elsa screamed in denial and agony. Now it was her turn to feel the rejection of a mate. Shields wrapped around her, bound her tightly and pulled her in towards Lily who held her dearly and tightly and rocked her weeping body. "I'm sorry Elsa." Lily whispered, tears in her own eyes.

Joseph he looked back at the king who was dearly trying to erect a shield for himself. "Your shield will be too weak against a mountain; you'll tire quickly when the weight collapses on you as mine would as well."

"I am strong!" He cried. "I can beat you. I am strong. I am strong."

Like a mantra the king repeated the words again and again as the mountain fell from the sky, and the trees plummeted down. He repeated it over and over and over as he saw the water flood downwards and the heavy stones and rocks hit at his flimsy shield. The king held on for a little minute, he held at bay his own death... for a few minutes anyway....

Epilogue

He thought death would be swift. He had prepared for it. He felt so weak with his blood having been drained by the King's magic but he was confused.

Looking up there was water float around his head. He saw it ripple and fade away. He was lying down, he knew that much, and he was weak, drifting towards unconsciousness. The trees and stones were floating alongside of him and he knew the mountain would be as well; oddly enough his body didn't feel beaten up by them. It felt the sharp, stinging pain from stab and claw lacerations but not the dull ache brought on by blunt earthen objects. He didn't understand, he had used every single ounce of strength, energy and power to achieve the end and while he was laying submerged in water, he was not dead.

And he was still breathing…?

He tried to move his arms but he was too exhausted for that. He still hadn't figured it out why he felt himself floating away. He saw the wave of the water above him, it didn't look blue, it looked a little on the grey on side, and it gave way easily to his body even as it moulded to him. Nothing hindered his glide under the water and he saw the sunlight trying to pierce through the liquid. The rays were able to show him how close to the surface he was. He was almost there. With furrowed eyebrows and a groggy mind he tried to work it all out. This death was puzzling, he didn't understand... until he saw the enchantress' face above him.

He had a shield of his own. With no magic left inside of him, for the time being, he knew this shield was not of his doing. They must have rallied together, combined their own magic; he knew it to be a joint effort simply because he knew them not capable of such a feat on their own. A shield was one thing, a projected shield another but Joseph had specifically brought down the heaviest things, just to make a projected shield impossible. He had underestimated them, or maybe he just never really believed the true extent of friendship.

He started to try and feel the shield around him and pin point just who exactly was saving his life, the evaluation was a little daunting. All the enchanters, all the sorcerers, even Perttu and Lily had joined together in the effort. But what really touched his heart was that those who had been fighting, the one he had promised change to and shown the white days to, were all adding their power. There was only a few of the soldier vampires that hadn't tried to help but he chuckled weakly to himself, you can never have everything. What mattered was, because of his own friends, and the majority of the fighters, he was surrounded by a pale pink bubble. They hadn't let him die.

His eyes were closing and he struggled to keep them open.

"Rest now, Joseph, you accomplished a lot today, take rest."

Too weak to do anything else he let his eyelids slide closed.

Days passed and they bathed him daily, they changed the dressings to his wounds and Perttu religiously forced his own blood down Joseph's throat in a bid to nourish and strength him. Still Joseph did not wake up.

"He gave everything of himself to stop the wars Perttu. He needs to build himself up again." The enchantress tried to reason with him.

"I feed him twice a day and it won't work!"

"It is working. He had a little colour back in his cheeks." The enchantress left the tent that Perttu was sat in and he felt a little alone as he was sat on the edge of Joseph's camp bed. "You're an idiot." He said to Joseph. "Why did you do that? Why was that your only way? Didn't you think of us? I thought I had lost you. I thought I'd have to scour the clearing for your body when the water had subsided. Damn it, Joseph I was scared you really were going to die! None of us knew if our shield would be strong enough! You idiot Joseph!"

"Perttu, stop."

From the corner of the tent came tiny, broken hearted whisper of a woman he had seen only once. Whipping his head around Joseph saw Elsa, she was huddled in the corner with her knees to her chin and her face was stained with tears.

"I'm sorry Elsa. I shouldn't have shouted at him. Especially since he isn't awake to hear me anyway."

"It's my fault he did that. I didn't wait for him. He left me a note asking that I wait for him but I didn't. And now he won't wake up because he tried to kill himself."

"He tried to be all noble and sacrifice himself." Perttu shook his head. It was a good gesture but in the end it felt… it felt as if they had had a lucky escape in saving him. "I love him for his strength. I know what lengths he'll go to now and I can try to protect him from himself in future. In the end though I will always have to live with myself knowing that I called him my brother and still never knew that he was tormented inside his own head. I never knew what it was he saw when he closed his eyes. I never knew what the white days did to him. I guess I also feel like I failed him."

"He wouldn't have wanted any of us to feel like this." Elsa reasoned, though it didn't stop how her own emotions from weighting her down.

"He wouldn't, but he can't magically stop my guilt, or my sadness. That's one thing his magic won't do." Sighing Perttu stood. After nodding to Elsa he left the tent, he needed Lily; he wanted some comfort and his Bride would give that to him.

Elsa was left alone with Joseph and she didn't move from her corner. Instead she began sobbing again, little coughs delicately interrupted this weeping but everything was silent. The soft crying was the first thing he heard. It hurt to hear, his chest ached at the sound. He was slowly coming back to consciousness and in utter confusion he wondered where he was and what he was doing in so much pain despite lying in something more comfortable than he was used to.

"Stop it." He called out to the weeping person. "Don't cry."

"... Joseph? Joseph oh my gosh, you're awake!"

He hadn't even opened his eyes but the first thing he felt was pressure on his torso and hands around his back and the first thing he saw was hair. Lots and lots of bushy hair and he squeezed his eyes hut before squinting upward to decipher whose hair it was.

"Oh Joseph, I'm so sorry, I'm sorry I never came to you. I'm sorry, forgive me, please I'm-;"

"Three sorrys and I haven't even taken three breaths yet."

Gently he pushed the woman away from him and stared at her confused. Who was she? She looked familiar. She felt familiar. She... she was silently crying now and it ached inside his chest. If it hurt to see someone cry then it meant she was his mate... his mate...... Elsa. Everything came flooding back in his mind, his memory temporarily clouded suddenly opened up and he remembered everything. She hadn't come for him until it was too damn late.

"I'm sorry." She said again.

"It's ok. It's not too late anymore, I'm not dead."

"No, no you're not. They shielded you. They saved you from your own magic. Joseph I'm so -;"

"Stop apologising. It's all alright. I knew you couldn't wait for me, your society is a little pushy on the marriage front." He chuckled a little and immediately felt weak.

"You need to sleep." Elsa said, she wrapped her arms once more around his healing torso and hesitantly lowered her head until it rested on his chest. When he didn't object she closed her eyes as well. "Sleep Joseph."

"Will you be here when I wake up?"

"Yes, I'll be here. I'm never going to leave you. Never."

When he woke up again he felt her lying on his chest and smiled. She hadn't left him. Slowly he lifted a hand and stroked back her hair savouring the feel of the silky strands. She didn't stir.

"She hasn't left your side." Turning Joseph saw Perttu by the curtain.

"What happened Perttu?"

"You were an idiot, nearly killed yourself. We combined our magic, each giving you a layer of protection. Thankfully there were a lot of us to create a shield thick enough to keep you safe from all that stuff. You gained a lot of supporters from the vampires you stopped fighting. They joined in as well, Joseph. They gave protection. We stopped you from being crushed to death or drowning but you were weak, you've literally used u every ounce of energy you had and you had been stabbed straight through many times. You were bleeding out."

"I have a lot of people to thank then."

"If you want to condense my long winded explanation." Perttu chuckled a little and came walking over to Joseph. "Why did you never tell me you couldn't sleep with the memories?"

Just at that moment the tent opened and Niklas popped his head around. On seeing Joseph awake he walked in, closely followed by Jaol who wore a relieved smile.

"Joseph!" He cried. "We worried."

"I... Thank you. You helped to save. I honestly didn't think that... I didn't think you would go to such lengths... I-;"

"Stop there Joseph." Jaol was shaking his head. Niklas pulled up a chair and put his fingertips together in a contemplating manner. It was Niklas who sat forward and studied Joseph intently before answering.

"We were tasked to be your 'holders' Joseph. That doesn't mean we were there only to keep you from hurting others; we were also there to save you from yourself, if the time came to it. We know what power does and we knew eventually you might feel backed into a tight corner."

"Don't thank us Joseph." Jaol's smile had gone. "We owe you for our lives as well. Our actions are balanced."

Still wanting an answer Perttu squirmed a little, careful not to wake Elsa up. She was exhausted from staying away, tending to Perttu and crying to herself constantly. "Joseph?"

"Because it wasn't your burden to have to deal with."

"I could have helped you."

"I didn't want you to think of me as weak. Or for you to feel sorry for me because of what I lived through. I wanted you to be as carefree as you always have been not fretting over my nightmares. Especially since you have children now, I wanted you to have as little to worry about as possible, because I know kids give you grey hairs easily."

"I don't have grey hairs!"

They laughed at each other but the seriousness was still in their eyes. The tone of their reunion was one of seriousness and there wasn't much room for jokes and light-hearted conversation. Perttu wondered how to explain the honour that had been given to Joseph and desperate to show how proud he was he grasped hold of Joseph's forearm in the age old meaningful embrace.

"The enchantress has done something for you."

"What?"

Joseph's curiosity rose and he stared at Perttu looking for answers. "She has suggested that you be a leader. Not in an army anymore, not in fighting, but as a liaison. As someone who goes from clan to clan listening to what everyone wants and trying to reconcile the vampire species. The idea is to produce solutions and stop the wars before they even begin. She wanted you to be a diplomat and she even went so far as to suggest that I might be able to help you."

"What? That... it sounds very idealistic but who would want me to muscle in on their clans?"

"Every vampire who saved your life out there. Every vampire who saw what it was you saved them from. She spoke to them yesterday morning and they agreed to it a few hours ago. If you agree, the position is yours... and mine. There's a whole species of us Joseph and I guess we do need someone to lead us, at least a little."

Joseph looked at Elsa, still asleep on his chest. "She said she wouldn't leave me."

"And she hasn't. She knows what it is the Enchantress wants you to do. She thinks you can rise to the occasion; 'impressively' was the word she used."

"She doesn't know me."

"She wants to. Don't be hard on her; she had a lot of family pressure. Lily told me that she disobeyed me and instead of going home, as I told her to, she went to fetch Elsa for you. She found Elsa collapsed on the floor after throwing up. She talked with her throughout the night but Elsa was scared of upsetting her father. On the day of marriage she got dressed but threw up again just before going to the church and Lily came up to her, to help clean up. Elsa changed her mind then, she knew her body was rejecting the human ceremony so Lily used a lot of magic to try and get them both down in time. They only just made it."

"I'm glad she did come to me though, even if I had to tell her to go."

"She is here now, that's all that matters. This is your chance at love. Grab it with both hands, you can be happy now. Sleep some more, for now, Joseph, you are still very weak."

"I don't want to."

Elsa moved around a little, her body wriggled for a second before her arms tightened around his chest and her head nuzzled further toward his throat. She seemed to be looking for comfort and feeling compelled he wrapped his arms her and hugged her tight. She leant into him as soon as he put his arms around her back and with his hands splayed wide across her small frame he looked back to Perttu.

"She'll be here when I wake?"

Perttu patted him on the hand and got up to leave.

"It looks like Elsa isn't letting go."

"Aye boy," Jaol said, standing to leave as well, "You finally got the girl."